THE SUMMER PROPOSAL

PART OF THE SUMMERS IN SEASIDE SERIES

AMANDA SHELLEY

Visit my website at
www.amandashelley.com

CONNECT WITH AMANDA SHELLEY

Want to be the first to know about upcoming sales and new releases? Make sure you sign up for my newsletter as well as connect with me on social media and your favorite retail store.

Website:
www.amandashelley.com
Newsletter:
https://geni.us/AmandaShelleyNL
Facebook:
https://www.facebook.com/authoramandashelley/
Instagram:
https://www.instagram.com/authoramandashelley/
Reader's Group:
https://www.facebook.com/groups/AmandasArmyofReaders/
Tik Tok:
https://www.tiktok.com/@authoramandashelley
Amazon:
https://www.amazon.com/author/amandashelley
Goodreads:
https://www.goodreads.com/author/show/19713563.Aman
da_Shelley
Book Bub:
https://www.bookbub.com/profile/amanda-shelley

ABOUT THE BOOK

My sisters are dropping like flies.

They're falling in love and having the time of their lives.

Don't get me wrong, I'm ecstatic for them. I love seeing them happy.

But I'm not ready for that type of commitment.

I can't even keep a plant alive, let alone find someone worthy of getting past a third date.

As the only sister done with school and single as a pringle, I have to do something fast, or I'll be my matchmaking aunt's next victim.

When Jax's drummer joins him for the summer and needs some help with his image, I make him a deal he can't refuse.

All is perfect—until I realize my summer proposal has one minor flaw.

Our relationship may be a sham, but there's nothing fake about my feelings for Finn.

Chapter 1
Raven

"Mmmm... Right there," I murmur as Brody kisses that fail-proof spot on my neck, making shivers run up my spine. Knowing this is just what I need, I pull him close, pressing my body against his.

"Oh... Raven..." he rasps, trailing kisses along my jaw. "I..." He starts but when his lips meet mine, I deepen our kiss, cutting off all verbal communication.

I'm not interested in conversation. I just want to get lost in him.

Thankfully, he takes the hint.

As one of his hands slides to the base of my neck, the other slips down to skim along the hem of my shirt, trailing across my lower back. Goose bumps erupt, and my anticipation grows.

God, it's been way too long. I've missed this.

Craving the feel of his skin on mine, I tug at the back of his shirt.

When Brody—*or is it Brady*—breaks our kiss, I practically cry out in protest.

With a wicked grin, he simply reaches behind him and pulls his shirt off with ease and tosses it onto my living room floor. "This what you want?"

Nodding, I quickly rip my shirt over my head and step toward him.

Shaking his head, he steps back. "Give me a sec. I wanna enjoy *all* of you."

Running my tongue along my bottom lip, I tease by slowly swaying my hips. "Well... by all means..."

I don't miss the way his eyes widen for the briefest of moments, and he quickly inhales. I love how his appreciative eyes roam from my face, over my lacy bralette, swooping low across my hips. The lust in his expression makes me feel sexy as hell.

I watch wordlessly, and he takes another breath almost as if he's steadying himself. The electricity zooms between us, and my body floods, anticipating his next move. I can't wait to have my way with this man. His sexy smile proves he's totally on board with this.

Showing we're in sync once again, as I reach for him, he steps forward. Just as his hand rests on my hip, and his lips press against mine, the shrill of my phone fills the room. Unfazed, he pulls me closer, but the second the sounds of "Hey Soul Sister" by Train blasts, my mood is killed.

"That's my sister..." I say, breaking the kiss without a second thought.

Leaning in to kiss along my neck, he suggests, "Can't you ignore it?"

"No... it's after midnight in New York. I've gotta take this."

Swiping my phone, I say, "Sloane?"

"Ohmgee Raven..." she practically screams into the phone.

"Give me a sec..." I quickly interrupt.

Whatever it is, she deserves my undivided attention.

Quickly grabbing my shirt, I slip it over my head, then press my phone to my chest. Turning to Brody, I point at the door. "I'll catch up with you later."

Before he can say a word, I walk to the door of my apartment, open it, and wait expectantly. Frozen in place, his face morphs through many emotions. Eventually shock, then disappointment spreads across his features. His eyes narrow and lips purse as he nods once.

Without a word, he grabs his shirt and stalks through the door.

Good. We're still on the same page.

Once I've locked the door behind him, I return to my sister. "Sorry about that. What's going on?"

"Ohmigod, you're not going to believe this... Wait... Raven..." Sloane suddenly admonishes, "did you just kick someone out?"

"He was just leaving," I quickly lie.

I haven't heard from my sister in nearly a week, and there's no way I'm missing this call. Between her being on tour across the country with Jax and the time difference, not to mention studying for finals this week, it's been rough. Besides, she'll always come first.

"Oh, Raven..." she says on a heavy sigh.

Not wanting her focus on me, I quickly remind her, "You know it's nothing serious. When I answered, I thought you might burst through the phone with excitement. What's going on?"

"I'm engaged!" she screams so loud, I almost drop my phone.

"Ohmigod! I'm so excited for you!" I quickly amp up to her level of enthusiasm. "Congratulations!"

I knew this was coming but didn't know when. Jax reached out a few weeks ago, while Sloane was distracted with work. He wished I could be there in person to pick out her ring, but since they're touring the eastern seaboard, and I had finals, it just wasn't possible. Thank God for modern technology. He knew Sloane so well, my job was simple. We picked out a kickass ring, though I'm sure Sloane could care less in this moment. All that matters for her is being with Jax. The way this man loves my sister so completely makes my heart melt for her.

Before she can get off track again, I demand as only a sister can, "Give me all the details!"

"Oh, God... where do I begin?" Sloane practically sputters, which is hilarious because my sister is *never* at a loss for words.

"Start with the fact that you freaking said yes!" Jax shouts beside her.

"I've already told her we're engaged... that's implied..."

Without being there, I know she's swatting at Jax with one hell of an eye roll.

Through the phone, I hear a rustling sound, and I'd bet my last dollar he's pulling her in for a kiss. When she remembers I'm on the other line, her tone sounds rather dreamy for my serious sister. "What was I saying?"

God, I'm dying. Only Jax can make my straight-laced, prim and proper twin lose all train of thought. This is priceless.

"First," I chime in, "remind me where you are. I've lost all track of days with finals."

She starts to talk... but I cut her off. "Wait, let's switch to video. I've missed your face."

"Just look in the mirror, goofball."

Once we've connected, my heart swells. Her smiling face is radiant. Jax snuggles into her and between the two of them, their mood is infectious.

Not that I'd ever let Sloane know, but I've missed her like crazy since she's been searching for talent across the country while touring with Jax's band. I'm so happy that she and Jax are following their dreams, but it's not the same as seeing her every day. Thankfully, she's oblivious to my true feelings, and her focus stays on her.

In the most unlike Sloane fashion, she talks nearly ninety

miles a minute. "We made it to New York City last night. Jax and his band performed at Terminal 5. Afterward, Jax asked to go for a walk. Since we've never been to New York, I wanted to see Times Square and the Empire State Building at night. Of course, being the amazing boyfriend he is..."

"Fiancé," Jax interjects by pulling her in tight and kissing her neck.

"Ohhh... I like the sound of that," Sloane coos.

Before they get out of hand, I tease, "I know how *amazing* Jax is... Sloane, you're killing me... tell me what happened!"

Sloane laughs as her eyes roll to the back of her head. "Geesh... have patience..."

"That's usually my line," I mutter on a laugh.

"Oh, how the roles have reversed," Jax interjects as Sloane shakes her head with laughter.

"Anyway..." Sloane interrupts. "We were enjoying the view of Central Park from the observation deck at the Empire State Building... The view was incredible. You've got to see it for yourself."

"Sloane..." I prompt impatiently, making Jax laugh again.

"Well, Jax was snuggling me from behind and suddenly, he disappeared. When I turned around, I couldn't see him. Seriously, I almost panicked, but then I felt something brush my leg and looked down."

I gasp, knowing what's coming next.

Pointing a thumb in his direction, she continues. "There, this fool was on bended knee, reaching for my hand."

Jax caresses Sloane's cheek as he gazes lovingly at her and says, "I told her she may have discovered me as an artist, but when I found her, I quickly learned just how much I was missing in my life. She pushes me to be the best version of myself. She challenges me to break the glass ceiling I'd always held in place and with her in my life, I know I can conquer anything that comes my way."

"Then he pulled a freaking ring box out of his pocket and asked if I would spend forever with him." The way her voice cracks, I can tell she's on the verge of tears.

Of course, my nose tingles with the tell-tale sign of tears on the precipice. I can't be entirely certain, but my super-spidey-twin-sense tells me we'll both lose it before this conversation ends.

God, I'm so freaking happy for her!

Taking a deep breath, I swipe at my eyes and ask, "You really had no idea?" My sister can spot a plot before any of us could ever put it into action.

Shaking her head, her face nearly splits in half with a grin. "Nope. He caught me by surprise."

How the hell did he pull this off?

"Have you told anyone else?" I ask.

"You first... always..." she reminds me of our mantra growing up. "Want to stick around while we share our news with Lanie and Liz?"

"Are you sure they're up?" Jax asks, looking at his watch.

"They'll be up for this," Sloane and I say in unison, then laugh our asses off as my sisters connect.

Chapter 2
Raven

One month later...

"Hey, Liz, wanna ride to work?" I ask, grabbing a cluster of grapes from the bowl on the counter. Popping one into my mouth, I moan. "Mmmmm... these are good... Heading that way, if you need one." Not sure where Lanie found these, but I could eat the entire bowl if I'm not careful.

"Nah, I'm meeting up with friends before my shift." Snagging a grape from the bunch in my hand, she adds, "Erin's picking me up."

Lizzy just finished her freshman year at Portland State. To earn some extra cash, she's picking up an unexpected shift at Booked at the Beach. Between that and working part-time for a nanny service, it's hard to keep up with her.

I swear, I've barely spent any time with her since graduating last month.

I must find the time and fix this—no excuses.

"I'm so glad you're all finally here," Lanie, our oldest sister, interjects, stealing one of my grapes with a sigh. "Summers in Seaside just won't be the same without us here together."

"We haven't missed one yet," Sloane deadpans, then her tone softens. "Nana may be gone, but her legacy lives on. Trust me. Not a day goes by that I don't think of her."

"Same," I add wistfully. I'm sure we all miss her terribly. She was always there when we needed her and never failed to call it like she saw it. She was a hoot. What I wouldn't give to snuggle under the blankets and watch our favorite movies again.

Sloane pulls me from my trip down memory lane when she adds, "What's up with the smell, though?"

Wait. What's she talking about?

After a lengthy inhale, Lizzy chuckles. "No kidding. You and Ryan live here year-round, but it still smells the same as when Nana was alive every time I walk through the door. Just how many air fresheners did she have?"

Lanie shrugs impishly, and I press her to spill whatever she's holding back. "Yeah... what's up with that? Did she have a lifetime supply or what?"

Chewing on her lip, Lanie looks to Ryan as if her fiancé will save her.

Odd. What gives?

This house is sacred to all of us. We spent many summer and school vacations here. We stayed with Nana when Dad was deployed, so Mom could earn extra money as a traveling nurse. We loved our time with Nana, and it hit us all differently when she passed.

Lizzy interrupts my thoughts by throwing a grape at our oldest sister. "Geez, Lanie, what's up with you?"

Ryan chuckles as he wraps his arms around my sister, holding her in place. "In my defense, I didn't know the backstory or the significance. But when I saw there were only two cartridges left, I wanted to surprise Lanie with more of what I thought were her favorite scent. I couldn't find them in any stores, so I went to the powers of the internet."

Lanie's eyes roll to the back of her head. "Boy, did the internet have powers. This fool thought he was buying just an extra box or two but ended up buying a literal pallet. Wanting to surprise me, he had them delivered to his parents'. Those suckers blocked the driveway, *and* he had to get a freaking fork-lift even to move them into their garage before it rained."

Gasping for air, I sputter, "Are you serious? How the hell can you mistake a few boxes for a freaking pallet? That must've cost you a fortune."

Shrugging, Ryan nonchalantly says, "It wasn't as much as you think. With all the expenses of the wedding coming out, I truly didn't notice until they arrived."

Lanie tsks, "They might have been seventy percent off, but you should've noticed."

Reaching for a grape, he says, "At least I got free shipping," before popping it into his mouth.

The room fills with laughter as Lanie smacks him in the arm. "Free shipping or not, you should notice when *any* purchase like that clears your account. In just a matter of weeks, we'll be married. How am I *just now learning this about you?*"

"Hey now," Ryan protests. "You know I'm a much bigger saver than spender." Leaning in, he kisses her temple and pulls her close. "Between automatic bill-pay and being so busy with this project at work—I'm trying like hell to wrap it up before the wedding—it slipped right through."

Ryan's been working on a new housing development just outside of Astoria. To make a name for himself, he took on this project, growing his family's business exponentially after grad-uating last year.

"You'll get it done," Lanie sighs. "Aren't you doing the final punch list on that last house next week?"

Knocking on the counter, Ryan says, "That's the plan. I can't wait to have three whole weeks without major responsi-bilities!"

"Well, you've got the family descending in two. You might want to rethink that. You'll be running around like crazy, helping us get everything for the wedding ready," Sloane interjects. She's the planner of the family. With Mom working back east again this summer as a traveling nurse, Sloane's helping Lanie with all the wedding details.

Even though she's spending the summer organizing the music festival, finding new talent, and planning for her own nuptials, she'll no doubt have spreadsheets to keep us all on track, helping Lanie have the perfect wedding. Lanie may be older, but Sloane has always taken planning to an entirely new level.

"Oh, your sister put me on warning. Trust me."

"Hey... I offered to elope... but you wouldn't hear of it," Lanie interjects. "You can't say I didn't warn you about our family."

When Sloane growls, the room fills with laughter. There's no way in hell the two of them would elope. Family is way too important to exclude them.

"At least I no longer have to deal with the meddling mind of Aunt Mable. Thanks to Jax, I've got an amazing career, and I'm officially off the market." Looking at Lizzy, she smiles. "Don't worry. She'll never say a word with you still in college. She wants nothing more than for us to be strong, independent women, like Nana did. But Raven... well, she's fair game... now that she's graduated."

"Oh, I can handle Mable." I nod, knowing I'll be her prime target. "I still don't have permanent employment yet, so hopefully, she'll spend her time working her magic to finagle me a job, rather than playing matchmaker. God knows the type of job she'd pick for me... let alone a man."

Wanting to spend this summer with my sisters, I haven't been serious about the job market. Between Lanie's wedding and Sloane only being home through the musical festival, there's no way I wanted to start a new job, only to request time off. Right now, I'm getting by working at Hops and building my design portfolio with several freelance jobs.

I've worked my ass off for the last four years and unlike most graduates, I walked out of school with no student debt. I made applying to scholarships my bitch, and with a double major in graphic design and marketing, with a minor in communications, I knew how to craft the perfect essay.

"Speaking of the perfect man." Sloane grins at the phone in her hand. "Jax is almost here." Turning to me, she asks, "You sure you won't join us?"

I love my sister, and I adore Jax, but I'm not up for anything fancy tonight. They're meeting his grandparents in Portland to celebrate their engagement and his return home from touring the country. Besides, they need this time with his family, and I won't intrude.

"I'm good. I'm running a few errands then heading to Pop's to catch the live band tonight. Marnie's expecting me."

The blasting of a horn catches our attention.

Lizzy shrugs, then grabs another bunch of grapes for the road and says, "That's my ride. Gotta run!"

When she gets to the door, she hollers, "Sloane... Jax is here!"

"We've gotta meet your parents in a few," Lanie says, turning to Ryan.

In a matter of minutes, the room goes into utter chaos as they gather their things, then morphs into complete silence after the door slams. Popping another grape into my mouth, I chuckle as I mutter, "I guess it's a party of one for me tonight."

POP'S HOPS is packed when I walk through the door. I manage to snag a high-top table in the undercover section of the patio. The band is already playing, and Marnie is nowhere in sight. Pulling out my phone, I shoot off a quick text.

> Me: You still coming?

Marnie moved to Seaside a few years ago. We met when I worked at the ropes course last summer. She's recently broken up with her boyfriend and told me she could use a night out.

Glancing at the time, I swear she said she'd be here by now.

"What can I get ya, Raven?" Tonya asks with an eager smile. I love the way her blond hair piles on top of her head in a perfect messy bun. It uniformly wobbles when she leans in to place a coaster on my side of the table.

"I'll have a rum and Coke with an order of sliders and fries. Have you seen Marnie? She said she'd meet me here tonight."

Glancing around, she shrugs. "I can't say that I've seen her."

"Well, she's missing a killer set. They sound fantastic."

Glancing around, she smirks. "They can sure draw a crowd. You're lucky you got here when you did. I think it'll be a full house tonight."

"I've been telling Sloane about these guys. She'll have to catch them before she gets too busy with the festival."

"Can you imagine if they hit it as big as Jax? Joe's head will explode."

Knowing our boss loves to tease about giving Jax Cartwright his big start, we all know it was one-hundred percent Sloane. But he won't hear otherwise. There won't be a customer in sight that won't know about his hidden talent scouts.

"God help us all." I laugh.

Rolling her eyes, she chortles, "I'll be right out with your order."

After she drops off my drink, the song switches to "Teenage Dirtbag".

I can never NOT sing along to this one, so when the chorus hits, I belt it out with the rest of the crowd while the dance floor fills up.

I'm caught off guard when a guy walking by stops at my table and stares. "Holy shit. I think I'm hallucinating."

Hmmm... he's hot. His piercing blue eyes go wide as saucers as he looks me over from head to toe. Clearly, he's high or something. I've never seen this man in my life.

Before I can respond, his face splits into a wide grin as he nods. "Straight-laced Sloane is slumming it *and* belting about dirtbags?" Turning to the guy beside him, he says, "Hmmm... I never thought I'd see the day. Can you believe it? She must be sloshed." Darting his eyes from his friend to me, he asks, "Do you think she needs help? I've never seen her so... so casual."

The guy beside him quickly glances around the bar, searching for something. When his eyes land on mine, he asks, "Where's Jax?"

Clearly, they know my sister. Maybe I should play with them a little?

"He's in Portland."

His head tilts to the side, and his eyes narrow when they land on my drink.

But his friend says, "Mind if we hang with you? There's not much seating left."

Gesturing at the empty chairs around me, I shrug. "Not at all. Have you been in town long?" I wonder just how well they know Sloane. If I'm being her tonight, the more info on them, the better.

"We got in this morning. I managed to snag that cottage you

told me about, but Finn's shacking up at the Sandy Shore Inn until the end of the week when his place is ready."

Okay, so she knows them well. This could be tricky.

Sighing heavily, the man now known as Finn says, "Jax offered to let me crash at his parents', but I'm ready for some space between tours."

"I don't know about you, but I'm just glad we're no longer on that tour bus and get to sleep in a real bed. It'll be nice knowing where we are when I wake up for a while."

"No kidding." Finn chuckles and places his arms on the table in front of us. "Though this town could get small when we're used to a different city each night."

Damn, his arms are sexy. They're long and muscular with a few tattoos peeking out from the sleeve of his black fitted t-shirt. Is that a barbed-wire tat wrapping around his wrist? It's covered by a few silver bracelets, so it's hard to tell. When he flexes inadvertently, his veins morph into corded stone, like the statue of David. Inadvertently, he lightly taps to the beat and when I look up, I find his piercing blue eyes staring into mine expectantly.

Aww shit. He caught me checking him out.

What the hell is wrong with me?

And when did I become a fan of arm porn?

Tearing my eyes away from his, I look over at his friend. "Seaside might be a tourist town, but if you stick around long enough, you'll find out why the locals enjoy it."

The clueless friend says, "If the label has their way, we'll spend most of our time in a studio. I, for one, am looking forward to some serious R&R."

The band switches to "Counting Stars", and our attention's drawn to one of the few couples remaining on the dance floor. The moment the tempo of the song picks up, they light up the dance floor as if it's their sole mission in life. I've never seen two people twist and turn in such a synchronized way. They take swing dancing to an entirely new level. He somehow pulls her in, dips her back, then spins her away, only to grab her hands from below and flip her like a rag doll.

"I've always wanted to do that," I admit after picking up my jaw from the table when the man drops her to the floor, guiding her by only her neck. "How the hell does she not fall flat on her ass?"

"It's not that difficult," Finn says, drawing my attention to him with a shrug. "With a few simple moves, you can do most of what they're doing."

"Yeah, I'm with her on this, Finn. I'm certain I'd drop the girl if I ever tried that. I'll stick to playing the music, thank you very much." Suddenly, he stands, pointing toward the bar. "You want anything?"

"I'll have any stout they have on tap," Finn answers, then looks to me. "Want another one?"

"I'm good for now. But thanks."

The moment the guy I have yet to learn his name leaves, Finn leans in close, and I take in his sexy scent. It's a mixture of pure pheromones and spice. But shivers run up my spine when his deep voice asks so only I can hear, "Just how long are you planning on keeping up this charade?"

Pulling back to look him in the eye, I blink at his unexpected question. "What do you mean?"

"Certainly, you're not Sloane Lancaster. I realized my mistake mere seconds after meeting you. In fact, I'll bet the next slow dance that you're her sister Raven."

Interesting. Not many people who don't know us well can recognize us so easily. Especially since he's never even met me before. Now I'm even more intrigued by Finn and as much as I'd love to see how this plays out, I feel a mischievous smile spread across my face. "So... what gave me away?"

He looks me over from head to toe as he slowly takes me in. "First, I've never seen Sloane drink anything but wine or margaritas." His eyes continue roaming until they finally meet mine. As if he's challenging me, I watch his tongue slide along his lower lip and chin, jutting in my direction.

My body heats as he appears to contemplate his next words.

A long minute passes between us, and a lump forms in my throat. Eventually, I manage to swallow and prompt, "And second..."

"Well, second..." He exhales slowly. "I'm sure as fuck, the only man Sloane Lancaster would ever look at like that... is her fiancé Jax."

"What are you talking about?" I blurt out. I wasn't looking at him any way special. Clearly, he doesn't have a clue what he's talking about.

"Well, you looked at me as if I were a tall drink of water after a long set on stage." He pauses for a moment, then quickly adds, "Nope. That's not it. You looked at me as if you wanted to rip off my clothes and have your way with me. There's no way in hell Sloane would ever look at anyone but Jax that way."

He's not wrong. He is hot, and I would have my way with him. But she wouldn't. She's only got eyes for Jax.

But in an effort to save face, I quickly ask, "Just how many drinks have you had tonight?"

His friend returns, and Finn nods a thanks in his direction before returning his attention to me. "This is my first for the night."

"Hey, Ryker. Raven didn't get a chance to correctly introduce herself before you left. Sloane and Jax are *both* in Portland. I guess we're hanging with her infamous twin sister Raven tonight."

Infamous? What the hell has Sloane said about me?

Reaching his hand to shake mine, Ryker says, "Well, it's nice to meet you. I'm Ryker Jones. I'm Jax's bassist. I'm sure we'll be seeing a lot of each other if you stick around this summer."

"Oh, I'll be around. With Lanie's wedding and all my sisters in town, I don't have any plans of leaving soon."

Ryker takes a long swig from his bottle of beer and grins. "Well, it's a good thing we've run into you then. It'll be nice to know a few faces at the wedding."

Tonya halts all conversation by dropping off my food. Before flitting away to the next table, she quickly puts in an order for the guys.

Grabbing a fry from my plate, I look from Ryker to Finn. Finn's thumb taps the rhythm with the band on the table between us. "If he's the bassist, are you the drummer?"

Immediately, he stills. I don't miss how he darts his eyes to his hands before landing on mine. His lips twitch as if he's suppressing a smile, yet his eyes crinkle in the corners. "Yep. That's me."

That's it. He doesn't offer more.

Instead of elaborating, Finn leans back, crossing his arms over his chest. His eyes bore into mine. The longer he stares, the more I'm dying to know about him. When his eyes narrow, I can tell he's waiting for my next question.

However, I don't give him the satisfaction.

Turning to Ryker, I ask, "How long have you been touring with Jax?"

Ryker takes a swig of his beer, then slowly exhales. Pointing to Finn, he says, "We've been with him from the start of his tour. It was supposed to be just for the contestant tour from winning the contest. But when Jax kept topping the charts with his singles, we made it official and became his band last week."

Tonya arrives with their burgers and fries, interrupting our conversation, but the moment she leaves, Finn continues, "Thankfully, Jax was only obligated to his contract for one year after winning the contest at the festival. Now that it's almost up, he can produce the songs we've been working on while on tour. He's still with the label, because let's face it, Smash Waves Records would be fools to lose talent like him. But thanks to his new kick-ass lawyer, he now has his own official band and more rights to how his songs are produced."

"Sloane mentioned something about him finally having more say in which musicians he worked with. I know he's eager to write more of his own music," I add.

"We all are," Finn adds unexpectedly. "By no longer just being a set musician, we can all have a say in the direction our music goes."

"Do you write as well?" Sloane never mentioned anything about Jax forming a band, so this is all news to me. I'll admit I haven't actually asked, so I can't entirely blame her.

Ryker chimes in, "We all do. Thank fuck we're fire once we get in a room together, or we wouldn't even have made it here this summer. Traveling between cities with a new band can either make or break you. We've got a good thing going between us."

Fascinating. I'm clueless about the music industry, though I'm eager to learn more. "You both obviously write, but do you sing as well?"

They both nod, but Ryker says on a smirk, "Sure, we do. Who do you think sings backup?" Shaking his head, his expression turns stoic. "Seriously, Jax was born to be the front man. He just didn't know it until our girl Sloane wagered him into taking that risk."

Grinning, I laugh at the memory. "She told you about that, did she?"

Ryker shakes his head and grins. "I'm not sure how I'd feel

about meeting a woman who'd change my entire life's trajectory on a tiny little wager, all because I wanted to spend more time with her. But we wouldn't be where we are today without that little ultimatum." Taking a deep breath, he looks to the ceiling before shrugging on a slow exhale. "Though to be honest, I wouldn't be surprised if you saw one of us take a song now and then, if vocals call for it." Looking to Finn, he smirks, and an unreadable expression passes between the two of them.

Clearly missing out on the inside story, "What?" rolls off my lips before I can think better of it.

"It's nothing," Finn quickly dismisses.

But Ryker must think otherwise because he adds, "Don't let our boy Finn fool you. He's equally talented as Jax. He's a wicked wordsmith and has written a few well-known songs for other artists."

Now my interest is piqued. "Would I know any?"

"You might. I've spent a few years working in Nashville and got to work with some amazing talent. But we've talked enough about work tonight." Looking to Ryker, he adds, "I don't know about you, but after touring steady for the last six months, I'm ready for a break."

Okay. That was abrupt.

Before I can judge him too much, he turns to me and reaches out his hand. Tilting his head to the dance floor, he says, "What do you say I teach you some of those moves?"

"Wh... what?" I sputter, completely caught off guard.

Raising a brow, he stands with his hand expectedly outstretched. "What do you say, *Raven?* Are you ready for that dance?"

Chapter 3
Finn

I may have lured her out on the dance floor by reminding her of the little wager I was certain to win. But in truth, I want to know her better. I love Ryker like my own brother, but if I want anyone knowing about me on a deeper level, it'll be on my terms. I'd rather them know the real me, not my reputation. Don't get me wrong, I'm damn proud of what I've accomplished in my twenty-seven years. I truly have nothing to hide, but the more we hang out with her, the more I realize I'd rather learn about Raven, without Ryker's help.

I've quickly learned she's willing to try almost anything—once. Or so she teased like a vixen when I asked if she was comfortable letting me spin her around the dance floor. Some moves are challenging, but she lets me walk her through them and the longer we dance, the more her body relaxes into mine. Within a couple of songs, Raven's picking up moves I throw at her with ease. She spins and twirls in ways she swore she'd never manage.

We even attempt the neck dip she'd pointed out earlier. The moment I tell her she's completely in control with this one, I get her to grip my forearm. Placing my hand on her neck, I dip her down and back up with ease. We practice it a few times without a care in the world about who's around us. When we finally get to the point where I try it in sync with the music, her eyes light up, and she squeals once she's back on her feet.

"I had no idea that would be so much fun! What else can you teach me?"

She was hooked from there, insisting I keep showing her new moves.

Raven's intriguing. She's smart, and she keeps me on my toes. I'm relieved to know my instinct about her is spot on. She's witty, constantly speaking in fluent sarcasm. After spending time with her sister, I can see their family influences run deep, but in some ways, she's the polar opposite of Sloane.

Take her outfit alone. She's wearing a pair of black ripped jeans and a graphic tee that says, "Salty or sweet, I'm still a treat." That should've been my first clue she wasn't her twin. As we dance around the floor, she pauses momentarily and throws her long hair into the sexiest messy bun. I doubt she's wearing makeup, and I'm certain she couldn't give two fucks about what anyone thinks of her.

It's so refreshing. I'm sick of people putting on airs and only want to be with me as a step to fame or notoriety. We've managed to talk a little as we dance, but it's mostly superficial. Though I love how she catches little things.

When I complimented her in learning these moves quickly, she asked, "You pick up that accent in Nashville?"

"Not exactly," I admit. "I'm originally from South Carolina and moved to Nashville when I was nineteen."

Her eyes narrow, and she remains quiet for a few bars of the music. Eventually, she breaks the silence by asking, "Just how long have you been in Nashville?"

"I'm not there much anymore, with the tour and all."

Adorably, she rolls her eyes. "You know what I mean."

"Is this your way of asking how old I am?" I tease as I swipe a strand of loose hair from her face. "If roles were reversed... wouldn't that be considered rude?"

"I'm not ashamed of my age," she says indignantly. Then her eyes narrow, and I feel the heat of her gaze cross over my features. "Though, I'd be lying if I said it hasn't crossed my mind."

I quickly spin her away from me in time with the song, then pull her close. When her hand rests against my chest, she stares expectantly.

Damn. I could get lost in those hazel eyes. Raven's fucking breathtaking.

I've spent months with her sister, and I should be used to looking at eyes like hers. They sure as shit shouldn't be so captivating. This could go sideways in a heartbeat... especially since I've signed a contract with her sister's fiancé. But somehow... well, fuck... my gut tells me Raven might be worth the risk.

When her head tilts to the side and she refuses to break eye contact, I find myself giving in. "I lived in Nashville for nearly eight years."

Running her finger down my chest, she smiles wickedly. "For an older man, you've sure got some moves."

"Oh, I've got moves, *sweetheart*." There goes my Southern twang. "Are you sure you'll be able to keep up?" Without giving her a chance to respond, I spin her out. Laughter falls easily from her beautiful lips as I quickly guide her through a series of twists and turns, making our arms like a pretzel.

Raven's so responsive on the dance floor. By the time the band sings the infamous song, "Closing Time" after announcing last call at the bar, I'm shocked this evening has come to an end.

Is it really that late? I swear we just got out here.

After spinning her away once more, I pull her close as the

song comes to an end. Raven snakes her arms around me and says, "I'm not quite ready to call it a night... are you?"

"Not even close." I grin, liking where she's going with this. "What do you have in mind?"

Chewing on her bottom lip, for the first time tonight she hesitates. "Uh... we could go back to the house... but we'll have to stay quiet as everyone's likely asleep."

"Or..." I wait until her eyes meet mine to ensure we're on the same page. "We could go to my place."

A grin spreads across her face as she heavily exhales. "I like that idea better. I love my sisters, but I miss living on my own, ya know?"

Without a conscious thought, my hand cups her face, and I pull her in. For a long moment, the world stops, and we just stare at one another. It's been years since my need to kiss someone has been this strong. Raven has me wanting things I know I shouldn't. But for the life of me, I just don't care. I know we're in public, and I shouldn't even think about starting something I know I can't finish, but I can't help myself.

My need for her is too strong.

Leaning down, I press my lips to hers.

Instantly, her arms wrap around my neck, and I feel her lift up on her toes to offset our height difference. The moment her mouth parts, I swoop my tongue in to taste her.

God, she's magnificent. The chemistry that's flowed between us all night ignites the flame that's been simmering. There's no way I want this to stop.

Her nails scratch along the hair at the base of my neck, and my dick takes notice.

Fuck, this isn't the time nor the place for him to be so alert.

Reluctantly, I break our kiss, then lean my forehead against hers. Panting, I ask the only question on my mind, "You ready to get out of here?"

"I thought you'd never ask." She grins widely, taking my hand in hers.

AFTER OUR FIRST KISS, I swear Raven's more addictive than any drug. Each kiss, caress, and touch has me wanting more. I'm so lost in her, I'm not even sure how we make it to my hotel. My lips are on hers every chance I get. At every intersection, in the elevator, and again in the hall, we take advantage of each stolen moment.

By the time I kick the door to my room shut, our energy is combustible. We're nothing but lips, teeth, and fumbling hands as we tear at each other's clothes. The moment she's in nothing but her lacy bra and underwear, I groan in satisfaction. "God, you're beautiful, Raven."

My eyes slowly roam across her body, appreciating the view. From the curve of her hips to the way her breasts swell from the sleek black lace, she's even hotter than I could've imagined. Stepping closer, my dick hardens as I watch her eyes take me in.

She's clearly checking me out... and I like it.

Fuck, it's sexy the way her tongue slides along her lower lip as her eyes lazily peruse from my chest to my cock.

And damn, if the dirty bastard doesn't take this moment to twitch in appreciation. Yeah... you'll get your turn, buddy. First, we're taking our time to enjoy every inch of this stunning goddess.

As if she can read my mind, Raven's beautiful face stretches into a wide smile as she reaches for the fly of my jeans. Within seconds, she has them undone and dropping to the floor.

Not that I'm complaining. In fact, I love her directness.

Feeling her sense of urgency, I quickly step out, then kick them out of our way.

When the vixen reaches between us and cups my raging cock through my underwear, I know I've met my match.

"Hmmmm..." she coos, running a finger down the center of my chest. "I think I want to kiss each and every tattoo on your sexy body."

"Christ," I growl uncontrollably when she squeezes me gently before sliding her hand around my hip to grip my ass. "You're gonna be the death of me, aren't you?"

Arching a brow, she chuckles. "Would that really be a bad way to go?"

"You won't hear me complain." I smile in challenge.

God, I love a woman who isn't afraid to take what she wants. Her confidence is sexy, and I can't wait to see if there's a limit to her adventurous side.

Suddenly, my mouth is too busy for words. Kissing along her jaw, she moans my name and scores her fingers along my back in appreciation. The moment I kiss the soft space behind her ear, she grinds her body against mine and pants, "Ahhh... Finn... I need more."

Fuck, if she keeps gripping me like that, I'm going to lose every ounce of self-control I have left.

"Tell me what you want, Raven," I manage between kisses. She squirms like crazy when I slide my palm along her upper thigh to cup her mound. Running a finger along the seam of her now soaked panties, I tease, "You like this?"

Her grip on my back tightens, and she moans apprecia- tively. "Mmmm.... Yeah... just like that."

I don't need to be told twice. She tilts her hips, and I gladly stroke the sensitive skin along the edge of her panties. Heat radiates from her, and my dick twitches, dying to get into the action.

Nipping along her neck, I take my time. Sliding along her silky skin until my lips travel across the swell of her breasts. Words aren't needed because every hitch of her breathing and sexy little moans tell me I'm on the right track. Her bra does nothing to cover her excitement as pert nipples practically penetrate the lace. Standing fully erect, they practically beg to be teased. Sucking a lacy clad nipple between my teeth, I slip a finger under her panties and slide along her heat. If my mouth wasn't occupied, I'd smile at how her responsiveness.

"Fuck... I need more, Finn... Ahhh.... Just like that.... Right there..."

Her hips rock into my palm as my fingers dip inside her. Pressing a thumb to her clit, I create a rhythm that drives her wild. The harder she grips onto me, the higher I take her. She's a slur of syllables and moans out her pleasure. When her body stiffens, I know she's close. Tweaking her nipple just right, I insert a third finger into her dripping-wet pussy while quickly rolling my thumb over her clit. Keeping a rhythm that has her uttering curses and panting my name.

I don't stop when her body quivers. I pick up the pace when her fingers dig into my back, pulling me closer. I certainly don't stop when she arches into me and begs, "More... I'm so close."

Hoping like hell she likes this, I do the only thing I can think of as *more.* Keeping our rhythm in place, I use the only digit I have left to apply pressure on that bit of skin below her opening.

"Holy shit..." Raven pants, and I almost pull away. But then she sighs heavily on a moan. "Don't stop... press harder."

Her wish is my command.

Within seconds, she's coming undone and fuck, if it's not the most beautiful thing.

Her hair falls down her back as her moans get louder.

Suddenly, her body stiffens, and she bites down on my shoulder to muffle her screams. "Oh, fuck yeah... just like that. Ride my fingers... Come all over them."

Pulse after pulse, her orgasm clenches around my fingers like a vise grip, and it's all I can do to keep her upright as she rides out these waves of ecstasy. When I've milked every last ounce of her orgasm out of her, she leans heavily against me, trying to catch her breath.

After a long moment, she sighs heavily, "What did you do to me?"

"I'm only just getting started," I promise. Though when her legs wobble, I ask, "You okay?"

On a light laugh, she clings to me tighter. "You've made me turn into Jell-O."

"Well," I say triumphantly. "Let's get you onto the bed so you can relax."

Before she can move, I quickly lift her with ease and walk the few steps to the bed, then gently deposit her in the middle.

To my surprise, Raven doesn't let go of my neck. Instead, she pulls me onto the bed with her with a wicked grin. "I think I'm ready to have my way with you."

"Are ya now?" I smirk, loving the way her hands roam my body.

Dragging one hand along my upper thigh, she once again cups my balls and squeezes me gently.

"Careful now, Love," I warn. "You could barely stand just seconds ago."

Running a tongue along her lower lip, her eyes blaze with heat. "I won't need to stand for what I've got in mind," she says, pulling me in for a kiss.

The moment our lips touch, fire ignites throughout me, and I know I've definitely met my match in Raven. Her body comes alive as she presses close. Wanting nothing between us,

I reach for the center of her bra and have it undone in seconds.

When her beautiful breasts bounce free from their containment, I'm surprised to find a small tattoo that has been hidden along her rib cage. It's an elegant font that reads, *Be afraid & do it anyway.*

In my short time of knowing her, these words fit her perfectly. Now I'm curious to know if there are more. Kissing down her body, I run my lips along her skin and ask, "Got any more tattoos?"

A light laugh fills the room as she arches into the bed. "I guess you'll have to keep exploring to find out."

Damn. I should've guessed she'd say that.

But now that the invitation to explore her body is out there, I'm eager to find out.

Scooching down the bed, I kiss my way along her body. When I get to her waist, I take my time and drag my teeth along her hip bones and kiss along her inner thighs. When she squirms, I slowly drag her panties down her hips. "Don't see any tattoos here... Maybe I should closely inspect that tight pussy of yours. Do you have any hidden there? Perhaps there's one on your inner thigh..."

"You'll have to see for yourself," Raven sighs, as my thumbs part her and my tongue flicks along her clit.

"Fuck, you taste good," I groan, not giving a fuck if there's any more ink on her. Now that I've tasted her, there's no way I'm stopping until she comes once more.

"Ohmigod, Finn," she pants heavily as her fingers grip my hair. "That feels..." Before she can speak more, I suck her clit into my mouth and plunge two fingers into her wet heat. "Fuck... right there..." she begs as her hips rise and legs clamp around my head like a vise.

Flicking my tongue rapidly against her clit, I drag my

fingers in and out. The tighter her legs pull against me, the faster I move. I can't hear anything but my own heart beating through my ears as she absolutely goes wild beneath me.

When her inner walls tremble, and the grip on my hair tightens, I know she's close. She feels like she's hanging on the precipice of ecstasy but might need a final push.

With my free hand, I reach up to her nipple and run my thumb over it. Finding a rhythm with my fingers sliding in and out of her now dripping pussy, I curl my fingers so they press deep inside her. After a few strokes, I go for broke. Sucking her clit harder into my mouth, I pinch the nipple and plunge my fingers deep into her, making sure I curl my fingers up toward her g-spot and press against her front wall. In and out, her body clenches around me and quakes uncontrollably.

Warm liquid flows from Raven as she arches from the bed.

I hear muffled screams, but between the blood pulsing in my ears and the convulsions of her body, I truly have no idea how loud Raven is. My only goal is to help her ride out this orgasm to its fullest extent.

When her quivers subside, and her legs fall off my shoulders, I look up in time to see Raven pull the pillow from her face. When her eyes meet mine, a lazy smile spreads across her face. "Well, that was new... I think you're the only one who's played my body like it was made for them."

"You've only experienced my hands and my mouth... just wait until my cock has his way with you."

"Oh, Finn..." Raven says as she reaches for my face. "If I die tonight, tell my family I loved them... and I died so... so happy."

Chuckling at her absurdity, I shake my head. "You may be calling for God tonight," I say, nuzzling into her neck as I lie down beside her, "but I promise there will be no dying."

Chapter 4
Raven

The room is well lit from the crack in the curtain, and I'm still in a state of bliss when I roll over and stretch.

Holy shit, my body aches.

And fuck, the more I move, the more I'm suddenly aware of muscles I never knew existed.

But as memories flood back, you'll never hear me complain.

Last night was wicked hot. I don't even care that I may never be able to walk straight again. Being with Finn was so worth it.

True to his word there was, indeed, no dying involved. It was anything but death. In fact, I don't think I've ever felt more alive.

I'm certain Finn had me speaking in tongues as I hung on the precipice of ecstasy countless times before I inevitably succumbed to sleep. I'll never forget how it felt when his cock finally sank into me. With his eyes boring into mine, he bottomed out and groaned, "Fuck... you're perfect."

I know more words were said, but the moment he moved, I lost all train of thought. He played my body so well, I swear Finn was given a secret code that had never been cracked. I have never... and I mean never... come so many times in one night.

"Hmmm…" Finn moans as he snakes his arms around me and pulls me back into him. "Where do ya think you're goin'?"

Damn, his sleepy voice is sexy.

My first instinct is to keep moving, but when he kisses my neck and spoons me tighter, I find myself snuggling back into him. I guess I can give in for a few minutes longer.

"Well," I say on a laugh when he runs his fingers along my rib cage. "Some of us have to work today."

"You haven't gotten much sleep."

"And whose fault is that?" I quickly counter.

His husky laugh makes my stomach flip in anticipation as he tsks, "I seem to recall you being very satisfied last night."

"It was all right," I lie playfully.

Suddenly, my body's flipped, and I'm lying flat on my back, staring into Finn's heated blue eyes. In my next breath, his body settles between my legs, and his brows raise in challenge. "Last night was *just all right*, was it?"

Running his hand along my thigh, he cups my mound.

Fuck. I'm already dripping wet. My traitorous body acts as if he didn't wring countless orgasms from me throughout the night. My once-sore muscles are long forgotten. When he traces a finger through my wetness, my hips arch up to meet him.

The moment his fingers enter me, he cocks a brow and asks, "Does this feel *just all right*?"

Oh, it feels more than all right.

Sliding in and out, it's all I can do not to scream out the truth. I crave him more than my next breath.

My God, what is this man doing to me?

Biting my lower lip to keep from expressing just how right it feels, I simply stare into his captivating blue eyes.

"What time do you have to be at work?"

I hear words but can't comprehend them. I'm too busy enjoying the rhythm he's playing.

Closing my eyes, my body arches further toward him.

Then he stills and firmly asks, "Raven?"

"Huh?" He expects me to not only think but form actual words?

I try thrusting my hips into his hand, but the bastard just repeats himself, "Raven, what time do you need to be at work?"

"Not until four. Though I need to do a few things at home before I go in."

Finn's eyes glint with mirth. "Is that your way of saying I can take my time with you?"

"Uh, I'm not sure it will take long," I admit as his fingers gloriously resume their stroking. "You've already got me hot and bothered... Oh... right there... If you stop, I might just rip your arms off and beat you with them."

His deep laughter fills the room. "Fuck, Raven, you really are perfect!"

I'M RUNNING short on time, and when I finally do try to walk out the door of Finn's hotel, he's slipped on a pair of sweats that hang dangerously low on his sexy hips and insists on walking me out. He wanted to walk me back to the house, but God knows I'll never get to work on time if he does.

As soon as we're out the door, he pulls me back in for a quick kiss. "Hey, when can I see you again?"

Shrugging, I give him the most honest answer I can, "I'm not sure. Between work, my family coming into town, and the wedding, it's a bit crazy..."

He interrupts with, "I get it." And presses another kiss to my lips. "I'll see you soon though."

"Okay…" I agree slowly after he kisses me once more. "I've really gotta go."

After pulling me in for one last hug, he kisses my neck, then pushes my hips away and smirks, "Go… get your sexy ass to work so you're not late."

With an extra sway in said ass, I get about five steps away before turning my head to see his reaction. His heated gaze doesn't disappoint, so I throw in one last tease, "See ya soon, Finn."

It's only a few blocks to my house, but as I contemplate our night and how it just ended, I laugh. I still must be in a sex-induced fog. Clearly, under normal circumstances, I'd never commit to seeing someone so soon.

I'm not looking for a relationship, but one more night with Finn might be just what I need to get him out of my system. I'll set the record straight with him next time.

Chapter 5
Raven

The door to my room slams against the wall, and I instantly bolt up in bed.

Sloane rushes through, screeching like I haven't heard in years. "What the hell have you done?"

Accosted by her sudden rage, I match her energy by barking out, "The fuck? What's wrong with you? It's practically the crack of dawn, and all I've done is work late and try to sleep."

Sloane's eyes are wild as she waves a paper in my face. "This... this is what I'm talking about!"

Of course, she shoves it so close to my eyes that there's no way in hell I'm focusing. Ripping the paper from her hand, I glare at my twin. Whatever this is, it's huge. I haven't seen her act this unhinged since we were kids.

Without looking at the paper, I look her dead in the eye and say the only thing I can think of. Knowing there's no use saying anything if she's worked up like this. She's dead set on being pissed at me and until I can crack through that barrier of rage, I won't get to the bottom of what's bothering her.

I whisper, "Breathe. I'm not sure what has you so worked up, but we'll get through this. We always do."

She heavily breathes in and out. Her cheeks are pink, and if

I weren't her best friend in the world, I'd think she was plotting my murder.

Holy shit! What the fuck happened?

Slowly, I glance at the paper in my hand, and my eyes nearly bulge out of my head when I catch the headline. "*Jax Cartwright's Fiancée Strays Just After Announcing Engagement!*"

Then those creepy bastards have a photo of Finn pulling me back in for a kiss outside his hotel. It's sensual and clear as day what we've been up to. Clearly, I'm doing the walk of shame. My hair is tousled, and I'm wearing my clothes from the day before. But we're not doing anything wrong. We're both adults, enjoying one another.

Then I read the caption *under* the photo and want to find this journalist to throat punch them. "*Straight-laced Sloane slums it this Summer in Seaside.*"

How dare they write shit like this about my sister...

My eyes try like hell not to read the trash on the page, but that's like asking someone not to watch a trainwreck. My eyes just can't look away. Before I know it, I'm filled with rage, just like Sloane.

"What the actual fuck? Who writes this shit?"

For the entire article, they go on about Sloane's unkempt look. They made fun of my messy bun, ripped jeans, and graphic tee. Sure, it's not Sloane's typical attire, but I didn't look as hideous as they make out.

"Oh, the fuck they didn't..." flows from my lips when I catch the line "*Sloane's obviously Finn's new treat. Jax should reconsider his choice in bandmates.*"

My mouth hangs open in shock as I dart my eyes to my sister. I'm sure they're wide as saucers as I say the first thoughts in my mind. "Obviously, this isn't you."

"No shit, Sherlock." The words roll off her lips bitterly. "I was having dinner with Jax's freaking grandparents, and Jax knows better... But everyone... and I mean everyone..." she eyes me pointedly before continuing, "is waking up to this shitstorm in the tabloids. How did this fucking happen, Raven? You know I don't care who you sleep with, but did the two of you have to be so... so public about this? This is a nightmare for the record label with Finn officially becoming a member of Jax's band. Rumors like this could wreck their new album."

Stating the obvious, I point out, "Uh... obviously, you tell them the truth. Don't people know you're a twin?"

"There's no way I want them trashing your name. You don't do serious, and we all know that. I don't want you caught up in this. You didn't sign up to be in the spotlight. I knew what I was doing taking the job at Smashing Waves; you had nothing to do with this. Besides, showing up for a few publicity stunts may fix this temporarily, but rumors are out there, and the rabid fans Jax has acquired will still hold this against me."

God, even when she's mad, she's still looking out for me. So typical of Sloane.

"If they don't believe you, then fuck them. That's their problem. All that matters is that you and Jax know the truth."

"Raven, this goes beyond the two of us... you have to—"

Cutting her off, I quickly remind her, "You've never cared what people think of you. I certainly couldn't give two shits about what they think of me either. Let the label know you're a twin, and I'll set the record straight."

"You don't understand, Ray..." she sighs heavily. "The label is pissed Finn put himself into a position like this," she sighs heavily and looks to the ceiling, "I wouldn't be surprised if they've even talked about canceling his contract and replacing him as the drummer. With Jax's new single out and the fact that they just launched their brand as a band, this isn't the type of publicity they need."

"Clearly, you weren't involved in any of this. Can't we do something like being seen in public together... clearly, they'll see you have a twin."

Sloane worries her lower lip and squints at something on the wall, suddenly in deep thought. Knowing her, she's thinking six moves ahead for what we should do. Before I can push her further, there's a knock on the doorjamb, and Jax fills up the space.

"Hey... is it safe to enter?"

Throwing my arms up, I flop back on my pillow. "Might as well."

As he walks toward Sloane, he shrugs with a smirk. "I take it you've met my bandmates?"

"Jax!" Sloane admonishes. "So not helping!"

"What? Too soon?" he says, snaking his arms around her from behind and kissing her neck. "Babe, you and I know the truth. That's all that matters."

Her rigid shoulders relax, and she sighs heavily. "You don't understand, Jax. Tara is irate. She talked about dropping Finn from the label. It took me forever to get her to understand the picture was clearly of Raven. Even then, my boss wasn't fully convinced."

"That's ridiculous. Finn didn't do anything wrong. Sure, he slept with me, *your sister*, but we're both consenting adults and not attached to anyone."

Shaking her head, Sloane persists, "Facts don't matter in stories like this; appearances and especially pictures," she points to the paper on my bed, "tell a story that can't be untold."

"Has anyone thought to ask Finn about it?"

"About that..." Jax looks to Sloane, then to me. "He refused to comment on anything. He looked me in the eye and said he'd never do anything to put our band at risk, and that I'd have to trust him, but he wasn't about to drag anyone's name through the mud."

"What's the big fucking deal?" I shout to the room. "Obviously, he didn't sleep with you, Sloane. Everyone in this room knows it was me walking out of that hotel. Hell, if they looked at Sloane and me, they could probably tell from my ripped jeans alone. So, we had a night of amazing sex, so much so, I was nearly late for work, but big fucking deal. I get that the two of you recently got engaged and with you topping the charts in recent weeks, your lives are scrutinized beyond measure. But Finn and I didn't do anything wrong, and Sloane was nowhere near that hotel. We all know that. This... this entire situation is just stupid!"

"Wait..." Sloane gasps. "You stayed with him all afternoon?"

"Out of everything I just said, that's what you got out of it?" I ask, exasperated.

Clearly that isn't where she should focus her attention in this moment.

"Focus, Sloane."

Tilting her head to the side, she studies me. "Ohmigod, you said you had amazing sex with Finn... And you stayed... for the entire night?"

Ignoring my idiotic sister, I look to Jax, hoping he'll be the voice of reason. "For a smart person, she's clearly missing the point."

"Oh, come on. This is kinda a big deal for you."

"Yeah, not every day my personal life explodes on the interwebs and splashes onto tabloid headlines, putting someone's career in jeopardy. This is a huge deal. I had a great time with Finn, but as Nana would say, '*We've got bigger fish to fry.*'"

"I'm sure we can set the record straight," Jax says hopefully.

"Finn's coming over for the family barbeque later this

evening with your dad and his sister, Mable, coming into town. Let's let the PR team do what they get paid for. Don't you have a picture of the two of you somewhere? Maybe that'll be good enough."

Sloane groans. "That's a good start, but unless we're seen in multiple videos or photo ops live, people could say it's fake news or AI generated."

Jax pipes in with, "So we go on a couple of double dates and make sure the photogs are tipped off. Maybe we go out in Portland or someplace other than Seaside, so people don't think we're staying here the entire summer."

I'm willing to be seen with Finn in public if it can help my sister and the band. But a thought crosses my mind that might be the most obvious. "Uh... have either of you even asked Finn what he plans to do about this?"

Chapter 6
Finn

Not only are the paparazzi going crazy around my hotel, hoping to catch me in the act with the wrong twin, but now I'm sitting at the Lancaster family dinner where her father shoots daggers my way when he thinks no one's looking. It's clear he respects his daughter's choices, but like any father, I'm sure he'd rather not see her image splashed across the tabloids leaving a hotel room.

When Jax gave me the scoop about her dad just minutes before I arrived, I nearly shit myself. He's a freaking lieutenant colonel in the Air Force. He's been a pararescue pilot for the better part of his career. He's had Special Forces training. He knows how to hide a body, and I'd be nothing but a memory to my family should he choose to do away with me. Christ, I feel like a sixteen-year-old getting caught in the back seat of his parents' car with a girl, rather than the twenty-seven-year-old man who should know better about keeping my private life out of the public.

As a set musician, I never had to worry about photogs keeping track of me, so this newfound fame is nothing I've experienced. I haven't had the chance to talk much with Raven, but I do know she's agreed to be seen with her sister, Jax, and me to set the record straight about me having an affair with Sloane.

After having my manager and some execs at the label hand me my ass for causing such a PR nightmare, I came straight to this dinner, in hopes of talking with Raven and putting this fiasco behind us. Little did I know when I was invited, it included her extended family. It was bad enough meeting Lizzy, Lanie, and her fiancé, Ryan, but the hits just keep coming when her dad and his sister, Mable, arrive.

I nearly die on the spot when her father mentions seeing the headlines because he's flagged our band's name to keep tabs on Jax's success. I love that he's tech savvy, but have I mentioned I hate technology?

The sisters wasted no time setting the record straight about a misunderstanding at the hotel yesterday.

You could've cut the tension with a knife.

This will go down as one of the worst possible "meeting the family" scenarios ever.

Ten out of ten, do not recommend.

What sucks most about this fucked-up situation is that Raven is someone I could see myself dating. She's smart, sexy, and fun to hang out with. I know we've only spent one night together, but I'd love to get to know her better.

However, the cold shoulder I'm getting from her at the moment has me thinking she might feel differently. It's awkward as fuck having a huge elephant in the room. Like a neon flashing sign blinking, "Finn slept with Raven."

Fuck, everyone knows what we did last night. I'm like a fish out of water in this situation. If only we could talk privately. Though, it's practically impossible to get a moment alone with her. Between her sisters, Aunt Mable, and the guys from the band calling me away for one thing or another, I haven't been able to pin Raven down for the conversation we need to have.

It's driving me crazy.

With a beer in hand, her dad finally approaches. "How's it going, Finn? You get enough to eat?"

This conversation could go so many ways, and my stomach flips as I clear my throat. "Yes, sir. I did. Thank you for having me."

"It's on the girls' invitation that you're here. I had nothing to do with it."

Well, shit. What do I say now?

Thankfully, he must realize I'm at a loss for words because he asks, "So, how long have you been playing the drums?"

Can't say I was expecting that.

"Hmmm... let's see...I've been tapping out rhythms since I could walk. I was that annoying kid always drumming my desk in school. I think it was my third-grade teacher, Mrs. Welker, who suggested I should get a drum kit for Christmas, so I could put my talents to good use."

This at least earns me a laugh from Mr. Lancaster.

Is that what I should call him? Mister? Or do I address him as Lieutenant Colonel? Fuck if I know? There's no way in hell I'm calling him Mark. Sir comes naturally, growing up in the South, but I'm out of my depth when it comes to addressing active-duty military officers.

"Do you play any other instruments?"

My shoulders fall from my ears, and I feel the tension loosen slightly. I can handle this conversation. "I can play the guitar and piano, though my preference is drums."

"I've heard some of the tracks you've participated in. You all sound fantastic together."

Shocked at the compliment, I say, "Thanks. Jax, Ryker, and I are fire when we play together. I can't wait to lay down tracks on our first official album this summer."

"I'm coming back for the festival. Sloane's snagged me some tickets, and I can't wait to catch up with some buddies who've recently retired. Apparently, Jax is the new Harry Styles or something with the teens." He chortles once and shakes his head. "Thanks to Sloane, my buddy Harps is scoring big by getting his daughter Frankie tickets. Apparently, she nearly passed out when she found she'd also get to see you perform at Lanie's wedding."

"Jax has wicked skills. I've been playing for years, and I can't believe Sloane found someone as talented as him at an open mic in Seaside of all places. He not only has what it takes to be a musician, but he gets the music business in general. I know I'm biased, being his new bandmate, but he's the main reason I agreed to form Ruby Frax."

"Okay, I've been meaning to ask, what the hell is a The Ruby Frax? Is that some girl one of you used to date or something?"

Chuckling at his assumption, I assure him, "No... it's got nothing to do with a girl. Trust me. It's way nerdier than you could imagine."

"Nerdy?" Raven's dad asks in disbelief.

"You know Jax was finishing his degree in computer engineering while on tour, right? Well, one night after he'd been studying, we were trying to come up with a name for our band once the tour was over. Jax was spent after hours reading code and jokingly said, '*Don't look at me, or we'll end up being the Ruby Frax or something like that. I'm up to my eyeballs in code, and Ruby is all I can think of. For all I care in this moment, we could ship our names together.*'"

Confusion spreads across his features, and I almost laugh. "Ship?"

"You know, when you use parts of people's names to create a new one—like a couple name? Finn, Ryker, and Jax became Frax. It's not that creative, but Ruby Frax sounds like something that will stand out and set us apart from the competition."

"I like the name. But never could've guessed what it meant."

"Most won't. Trust me," I assure him. "But fans are on board with it so far, and we're getting some good publicity with the festival coming up in a few weeks."

"I imagine it'll be great exposure. Just look at what you've been able to do since announcing The Ruby Frax."

"If all goes well, we'll drop our first single just a few days after our first official performance as a band. Then we can build up hype for our full album."

"I'll admit, I don't follow the music scene. I just listen to what catches my ear. However, since Sloane started working at Smashing Waves Records, I've taken an interest in the talent she finds. Though with Jax in particular, I'll admit, I keep closer tabs on him. With the whole vested interest on his future and how it relates to Sloane."

When his eyes bore into mine, I see the double meaning behind his words as clear as day. He'll keep tabs on me, too.

Fuck, I really need to talk to Raven.

As if I've conjured her in my brain, her distinct laughter interrupts my thoughts, drawing my attention her way. She looks radiant. Her face lifts to the sky, and her hair cascades down her back as she belly laughs from across the deck. Lizzy's got her full attention, and I'll admit my curiosity is piqued. I'd give anything to know what's causing this kind of reaction. She's so fucking beautiful.

Clearing his throat, her dad regains my attention.

The moment my eyes lock onto his, he says, "I've been watching the two of you all afternoon. My job depends on me reading the room. I don't think the tabloids got *everything* wrong in those photos. You're clearly interested in her. Don't you think it's time she stopped avoiding you?"

My mouth drops open, and I'm sure I blink at him in shock.

I thought for sure he hated me. What man wouldn't hate the guy putting his daughter negatively in the limelight? That's one thousand percent deserved.

Placing a hand on my shoulder, he waits for me to close my mouth and really hear what he has to say. Tipping his head in her direction, he leans in and whispers so only I can hear, "Tread lightly with that one; she's tough as nails on the surface, but her heart is far bigger than she'll ever let on."

Chapter 7

Raven

I've been keenly aware of Finn's presence since the moment he walked through the door. I've also purposely been avoiding him like the plague because what the hell do I even say? I've agreed to public appearances to ensure the vulgar rumors about Sloane and Finn cease immediately.

To give my senses a break, I venture into the kitchen to help with the last bit of preparations for dinner. Of course, there's nothing to be done. Why couldn't my sisters leave me something to do? How else am I supposed to avoid both Mable and Finn?

The sliding door opens, and my heart thunders in my chest when I find Finn approaching alone. There's so much we need to talk about, but I don't know where to begin. With my family here, I'm not sure what we'll get in terms of privacy either.

"Can I get you anything to drink?" I offer.

Closing the distance between us, his masculine cologne makes my inner muscles clench. Damn, he's so sexy. Black jeans, fitted black tee, and black work boots make his rocker look complete. His tattoos peek out from beneath his sleeves, and I fondly remember running my tongue along them.

Has it really been less than twenty-four hours since I left his room?

"I—" I start, but I'm cut off by his words.

"I never meant to drag you into a PR nightmare." The sincerity in his eyes guts me.

"I doubt anyone would do that on purpose," I remind him, hoping he knows I don't blame him. "We can make a few appearances and clear up any rumors about you being with Sloane."

"I'm not so sure I want just a few appearances," he quickly counters.

Shit. That could be a problem for Sloane. "Well, my sister and I can be seen with Jax then, if you don't want to set the record straight. I'm not about to let her name get smeared for no reason."

Reaching for my hand, he shakes his head. "No... you don't understand. I think we should have *more* than a few appearances together."

Not entirely sure where he's going with this, I tell him a truth I should've started with yesterday. "I'm not looking for anything serious."

"It doesn't have to be serious, but you should know I'm not a player. I don't step in on anyone's relationship. I really like you and don't want you to think I'd be okay doing that to anyone, let alone a bandmate."

Still, there's so many ways I could interpret those words.

Before I can respond, he blurts out, "The label is on my ass to make this right, and I, for one, *never* want the word cheater anywhere associated with my name." His expression darkens. "You're the only one who can help me put those rumors to rest. Even if you'd prefer to just hang with your sister and Jax, can I be included in these plans to ensure to the world nothing nefarious has happened?"

"I... I don't know..." What is he asking? Does he want to spend time with me? Or is all this so he can clear both his and Sloane's name?

The sliding door opens, and my sister Lizzy and Aunt Mable walk in. "Oh, there you are," Mable says, oblivious to the tension in the room. "Burgers are ready. Lizzy, you grab those napkins, and I'll use the powder room."

Leaning in so only I can hear, the hairs shimmer along my neck and arms when Finn says, "You don't have to decide now, but please think about it."

Turning on his heel, he strides out of the room, leaving me with my thoughts.

"You okay, Ray?" Liz asks as she returns from the garage with a pile of napkins in her hand.

"I'm..." Hell, I don't know what I am, but this doesn't need to become her problem. "I'm good. I'll be out in a sec."

The moment I'm alone, I press my arms against the counter and lower my head. Taking a deep breath, I process what's transpired since meeting Finn. I don't do relationships, but for the sake of my sister, I think I might have to at least pretend to be in one.

Mable makes an appearance the moment I straighten up. "Oh good, I caught you alone. How are you holding out, honey? I've been thinking about you since your graduation. I met the sweetest boy earlier at the grocery store. He's home for the summer and just finished his degree, too. I think he'd be perfect for you. He's an accountant and has a great head on his shoulders." Then she cups a hand around her mouth and whispers conspiratorially, "He's not bad on the eyes either."

Holy shit. Even with all the drama today, this takes the cake. Why on earth would she think I'm interested in dating a complete stranger?

"Oh, don't give me that look, Raven Rene. I'm not dead yet. Just trying to find a nice boy for you to settle down with."

"Mable," I groan. "I'm not ready to settle down. I literally just graduated, and I'm focusing on my career."

"Sweetheart." Mable's eyes are warm and filled with love. I know she doesn't mean any harm, but she just doesn't get me either. Rubbing a hand along my shoulder, she uses the other to place a finger under my chin. "I love you like you're my own grandchild. I know your heart is larger than most can handle. Like my sister, Jane, I just want to see you happy."

"I am happy," I assure her.

With a wicked smirk and a wink, she says, "You may think you're happy now, but I'm certain there's a plan in place for you to meet the man who won't try to tame that wild heart of yours. He'll merely complement it and enjoy the ride along with you."

To pacify her, I relent, "You may be right, but I'm not in any hurry to meet him."

The sliding door opens again and this time, it's Dad who pops his head in. "You two gonna eat? We're waiting for you to start."

Giving my hand a squeeze, Mable walks out of the room with a smile.

Once I'm outside, I slide into the open spot next to Finn on the picnic table.

His face splits into a beautiful grin when I nod and whisper, "I'm in... but I have some stipulations."

Rolling his eyes, he grins. "Of course you do; lay them on me."

"One, we keep up the charade of *fake* dating through my sister's wedding and my matchmaking Aunt Mable is out of town."

"And two?" he asks, his face stoic and unreadable.

"Two, we stay exclusive, so you won't have to deal with a cheating scandal under my watch. I despise cheaters and won't take part in it. Third, we make this believable. My sisters are awful liars and if this isn't believable to them, there's no way we can clear your names with the public. I refuse to let anyone think less of Sloane."

"Anything else?" he quips.

Racking my brain, I can't come up with anything else. "No... I think that's about it. What about you?"

Glancing around the table to those around us, he whispers, "We can deal with my terms when we're alone."

Why the hell did that promise just make my body heat?

Chapter 8
Finn

Between our studio time and everyone's work schedule, I haven't seen much of Raven for the last few days. This week has been brutal with sessions, but we've managed to make use of our time. We're on track to finish this album with plenty of room for engineering to put on the final touches before release day.

Since the studio had a scheduling conflict, Ryker is using this time to fly home for the weekend. I dropped him off at the airport earlier, and I'm on my way to meet up with Jax and the girls in the Pearl District for dinner and a show. Nick Conners, from the band Riser, is performing solo tonight to an intimate crowd, and it'll be a great way to casually get some publicity without having it look staged.

Knowing I'd be here for the summer, I bought myself a used mid-sized SUV. It's nothing to write home about, but it's got great miles, is in great condition, and will easily haul a drum set, if necessary. Depending on how long we stick around, it'll be great when winter hits, too. There may not be much snow and ice along the Oregon coast, but those rainy days everyone talks about are real, or so I'm told. I'd feel much safer in a vehicle that can handle the vast terrains of the Pacific Northwest.

Snagging a parallel spot near the venue, I quickly park and

make my way to the line forming outside The Purple Pickle Bar & Lounge. Not seeing Jax or the girls, I pull out my phone and shoot off a quick text.

Me: Just arrived. Are you inside?

Jax: Grabbed a table on the left toward the stage. Left your name with the bouncer to guarantee access. It's a sold-out show.

Me: Got it. Thanks

The moment I get inside, I spot Raven and beeline it to her. They're sitting at a high-top table and before taking the seat next to her, I wrap an arm around her shoulder.

"Hey, Raven. It's great to see you." Without thought, the moment her face turns toward mine, I lean and press my lips to hers. Kissing her feels so right. It's as if no time has passed, and we're back in my hotel.

Damn, she tastes better than I imagined.

Remembering where we are, I keep it brief. When I pull away, I notice her lipstick is smudged, so I fix it with my thumb. Fuck, those lips have me wanting more. It would be so easy to get lost in her.

Her smile shines bright as she pulls away. "Hello to you, too, Finn. Did you get Ryker off okay? I wish I didn't have to cover the afternoon shift, or we all could've ridden together."

"It's all good. Maybe I can convince you to ride back with me and keep me company."

"It's the least I can do." Raven smirks. "I'm the one who caused you to drive alone in the first place."

Needing to touch her once more, I rest an arm across the back of her chair and lean in. "Have you eaten?"

"We ate on the way," Jax admits. "Though those food

trucks not far from here are bound to be open when the crowd lets out. You wouldn't have to twist my arm to stop by."

"Oh, that sounds great. I haven't been there in years," Raven pipes in.

Since this is an intimate show, there's no opening act for Nick Conners. The lights dim, and he walks on stage with his guitar. No big fanfare or pomp and circumstance. He simply starts into his first song. I've worked with Nick in Nashville, and he's a great guy. He does shows like these to keep grounded. He and his band, Riser, have been big for a few years. From what he's told me, sometimes he just wants to be a guy with a guitar.

With his band or flying solo, the energy Nick brings to the stage is infectious.

"Hey, let's squeeze together for a group selfie," Sloane offers when he finishes his first song. She takes a few shots, then taps away on her phone while Nick talks about how important it is to play here in his hometown. "There." Sloane beams. "I've posted on all socials. The PR team at Smashing Waves will work their magic to get these shots to the right people."

Turning her phone to her sister and me, she says, "I hope you don't mind; I took a couple of candid shots when you first arrived. I don't know about you, but I'm ready to set the record straight. These rumors are getting ridiculous."

The heated look in my eyes when I greeted Raven is evident. I'm clearly only into her. The shot is wide enough that Jax is on the edge, smiling wide. Clearly, I'm not stealing his girl.

"It's time to get out of work mode," Raven deadpans. "I, for one, just want to enjoy the music."

"I'm totally on board with that." Jax grins, pulling Sloane into him. "Put that phone away and turn off that brilliant brain of yours."

Wanting to give them their privacy, I turn my attention to Raven and ask, "Wanna dance?" There are only a few other couples out on the floor, but if our time is limited, I'm making it count.

A radiant smile lights up her face. When she reaches for my hand, my entire body heats in anticipation. "I'd like nothing more."

Within seconds, we're on our feet, moving to the beat. I still can't get over how responsive Raven is in my arms. I turn, she twists; I lean, she dips; I pull her close, she melts against me.

Inhaling deeply, I catch a slight scent of the ocean breeze mixed with her perfume, and it's like an aphrodisiac I never knew existed. It's sexy and sweet, and I'll be dammed, but I just can't get enough. The moment her fingertips scrape at the base of my neck, my body hums with an energy I've never experienced. The way her head fits on the indent of my chest, I swear this girl was made for me.

Wait... what the hell am I thinking?

Shaking my head, I laugh at the audacity of that thought. We just freaking met.

"Hey," Raven says on a laugh, regaining my attention. "What's going on in that head of yours?"

"Just thinking about how much I'm enjoying this moment." That isn't a lie, but there's no way I'm copping to those thoughts this soon.

Tilting her head to the side, her eyes narrow. "You sure that's all it was? You went from smiling like a loon to pensive in a nanosecond."

Note to self... she's perceptive.

Spinning her out, I grin at how easily she follows my lead. "Nope. Just lovin' how well you move." I twist her in and out of a pretzel-like move, then pull her close again and tease, "It doesn't hurt that you smell good either."

"Well... uh... thanks. Not quite sure how to take that... But for the record, you don't smell so bad yourself. I..."

Whatever Raven's about to say when Nick Conners booms through the speaker is cut off. "As I live and breathe... is that Finn McGowen out on *this* dance floor? Ladies and gentlemen, please excuse me for a second. I think I'm hallucinating."

Turning my attention to the stage, I grin at the jackass, ruining this moment. "Hey, man, it's been a minute."

To the crowd, Nick says, "We've got an amazing drummer here, ladies and gentlemen... scratch that... He can play almost any instrument he touches. He was a huge help when I recorded in Nashville a few years ago... Man," he says, hopping off the stage. "It's good to see you."

Reaching out, he shakes my hand, then pulls me into a bro-hug, thwacking my back three times before releasing me. Looking toward Raven, he grins like the Cheshire cat.

"And who do we have here?"

Without skipping a beat, Raven reaches out her hand and says, "I'm Raven. It's so nice to meet you."

"Well, Raven..." Nick exhales theatrically. "In all my years of knowing Finn McGowen, I've never seen him look at a woman the way he looks at you. I really hope I get to chat with y'all later after the show."

Then as if he suddenly remembers he's in the middle of a live performance, he grins. "Well... I think I should probably get back up there and finish this set."

Without skipping a beat, he returns to the stage and slips seamlessly into his next song. Raven hops up and down, clapping her hands together. "Ohmigod, I love this song. I had "Believe in Me" on repeat in high school. Not only did I just get introduced to Nick, but now he's playing one of my favorite songs. How the hell did this become my life?"

"Uh, your sister *is* engaged to Jax Cartwright," I point out on a laugh. "Aren't you used to being around famous musicians by now?"

Raven practically snorts. "Hell no! I spent the last year busting my ass to finish college. I don't really think of him as being anything special—other than the fact he lights up my sister's whole world. I'm not really impressed by fame... but..." she looks at the stage, "Nick Conners was on my wall growing up. It's a bit surreal."

"I get it. I was the same way when I met Stevie Nicks."

Raven gasps. "Oh, that must've been amazing."

"It was, trust me."

Nick starts into the bridge, and I reach for Raven, pulling her close so I can whisper in her ear, "With this being your favorite song, let's make some memories."

Chapter 9
Raven

My body pulses with energy as we walk to Finn's car. Nick Conners was on fire tonight. I'd only seen him in concert with Riser. On his own, he was so much more memorable. Though it might have more to do with the sexy man holding my hand as we walk down the street, than Nick Conners.

Leaning into Finn, I can't help but smile at how much fun this evening has been.

Thank God, when Nick stopped by our table during one of his breaks, I didn't say anything embarrassing. After my initial small moment of internal fangirling on the dance floor, I was relieved to find he was just a normal guy, who happened to be fucking amazing at playing music. I was captivated with each story he and the guys talked about. At one point, Finn teased him about going on tour again, and Nick just grinned like he'd won the lottery when he explained that he'd only be home through the summer, due to his growing family.

Nick may command the stage like the sexy rock star he is, but the man melted my heart when he broke out his phone to show us pictures of his family. The first was of his son, Jacob, and his very expecting wife Simone. Jacob is the most adorable five-year-old ever and their daughter, Emery, is the spitting image of Nick, with his beautiful smile and eyes. Apparently, they're expecting number three in the next week or so, or Simone would've been here tonight.

"Now, it's my turn to ask what's going on in that head of yours?" Finn chuckles as he wraps an arm around me, pulling me close. "I've never known you to be so pensive."

Inhaling deeply, I sigh. "Just thinking about Nick Conners."

Finn stops and faces me with a mischievous grin and a raised brow. "Somethin' I ought to worry about?"

As he waits for a response, he hits me with those penetrating blue eyes and brushes a strand of hair from my face.

Batting my hand at his shoulder, I laugh. "Ohmigod... No... Not like that, you dork. I just couldn't believe he's so down to earth and such a family guy. He's performed in sold-out stadiums all around the world and yet he finds so much joy in being *just a guy with his guitar*."

Yes, I use air quotes.

"It's so surreal." I shrug as if that will explain the thoughts swirling in my head.

"Don't get me wrong, there are many big-name performers who need to build giant mansions just to let their ego remain in the same room as themselves, but Nick's most certainly not one of them. In fact, none of Riser is."

"That's good to know. It would suck to think someone you idolized as a kid was nothing but a giant asshole in real life.

"Fame is fickle. Everyone handles it differently. I've been in the studio with all walks of life, trust me. If Ruby Frax takes off as well as I think, you have my full permission to smack the shit out of me if I ever become a self-absorbed asshat who acts better than he is."

I feel my eyes roll before I give them permission as a small laugh escapes.

Like that will ever happen. The man is nowhere near the egomaniac level I've heard horror stories about from Sloane. But instead of complimenting him, I smirk. "What makes you so sure I'll be around?"

"Well, your sister *is* marrying our lead singer. Where he goes, I'll be right along with him. I'm sure our paths are bound to cross, and somebody's gotta keep me in check."

Rather than thinking about the ramifications of that truth bomb—Finn will always be around—I playfully tip onto my toes and wrap my arms around his neck. "Well, it's probably important we get along then... you know... at least for the sake of appearances."

His eyes darken as his tongue drags along his lower lip. "Oh, I'll show you appearances, Raven... Trust me."

Before I can fully inhale my next breath, his lips crash onto mine, and his arms wrap tightly around me. We've been playfully skirting around the edges of this kiss all night. But until this very moment, I had no idea how much I've needed this man's lips upon mine.

Parting my lips, his tongue swoops in, deepening our kiss. My belly flips as tingles shoot up my spine, and the energy between us makes my entire body hum. I know I should hold back since this is only for the sake of appearances, but I can't find it in myself to do so. All that matters is how good it feels to be in Finn's arms. The warmth of his skin on mine makes my thoughts disappear as my body responds to each and every move he makes, making me want more.

Digging my fingers into the hair at the base of his neck, I'm startled when a blaring horn bleats mere feet from us, causing us to abruptly break apart.

"Holy shit, what was that?" I pant wildly as I dart my eyes around for the danger.

Breathless, Finn grins as he runs a palm down his jaw. "I'd say some jack hole was jealous."

Well, this has my attention.

"Of what?" I ask, clearly confused.

Leaning in, he kisses my temple. "Being lost in the moment with a beautiful girl."

"Oh, geez," I scoff at how easily that rolled off his lips. "Does that line really work for you?"

"Not a line, Raven. Let's get you settled into the car. We've got a long drive ahead of us, and you've got an early morning with your sisters."

I feel my mouth drop open as I silently process his words.

He takes my hand in his as we walk past a few more cars and stop in front of a black SUV. Instead of unlocking it, he turns to me with a grin. "Let me kiss you once more... for appearances and all... you never know who may be watching."

The moment my head tips in his direction, his lips return to mine, and I kiss him for all I'm worth. If anyone's watching, they'll certainly get a show. But the real question I have for Finn—is this really just an act?

WALKING INTO THE KITCHEN, I've got one thing on my mind—coffee and lots of it. My sisters and I have a full day with our final dress fittings and making decorations for Lanie's reception. The guys are tasked with making the arch for the ceremony and picking up a new grill for the rehearsal dinner since Dad insists on making his infamous ribs. With less than a week to go until the wedding, it's all hands-on deck until Lanie's big day.

Relieved to find a full pot fully brewed, I reach for a mug from the cupboard and fill it to the brim. Sliding it along the island, I place it in front of my favorite seat. Not only does it have the best view of the ocean, but it's where Nana always placed my food when she was cooking for us. Not that we had official seating arrangements, but I think this location kept me busy, as it was closest to the fridge and pantry should anyone need anything.

Speaking of pantry, toast sounds good. Sludging over, I grab the bread and peanut butter, pop two slices into the toaster, and wait as my breakfast cooks. I have no idea how long it will be until my family comes down, but for now, I'll just enjoy the calm before the chaos of the day begins.

When I turn around, there's a dark figure standing merely inches away. I nearly jump out of my skin as my heart catches in my throat, and a strangled shrill escapes. The moment I recognize it's only my dad, I reflexively bat at his chest. "Geez... make some noise like normal people!"

Chuckling, he pulls me into his arms. "Maybe you should be a little more aware of your surroundings, sweet girl, so I won't get the drop on you."

As my heart rate returns to normal, I snuggle into his infamous hug. It's safe and warm and smells like home. "Not all of us are programed to function at the ass-crack of dawn, Dad. Some of us need coffee first. Then I can dish it back like you obviously deserve."

I feel his laugh before hearing it. "Oh, Raven, I'm glad you think you can try."

Yeah, I know I'll never win against him. His years of training have made him stealthy. But he's always fun to tease. "One day, Dad, I'll get one over on you."

Releasing me, he reaches for a mug of his own. "You always do keep me on my toes. In fact, I'm surprised to see you up this early after getting in so late." Settling on the stool beside mine, he reaches for the bowl of fruit in the center.

Pulling one of his favorite lines, I shrug. "Couldn't waste the day." Grabbing the toast, I quickly spread butter and peanut butter on it. "Besides, my caffeine addiction takes priority if I'm forced to spend the day shopping and wedding prepping. I love Lanie to the ends of the earth and wouldn't miss this for the world, but you and I both know I need this if I'm expected to function today." To prove my point, I take a large gulp from my mug.

"How are *you* feelin' about everything? I haven't been able to check on you, and I'm certain that part is intentional on your behalf."

Leave it to him to see through my crap. Yes, I've been busy, but I've purposely done so. I don't like to burden my family with my problems. It's just not who I am.

"I'm good, Dad. Between freelancing, my job at Pop's, and helping Lanie with the wedding, I'm pretty busy." I'm sure that's not what he's referring to, but nothing I said was a lie.

Raising a brow, I can tell Dad chooses his next words carefully. "I know this year was rough on you being at school on your own... and now that Sloane's engaged, your culprit in crime isn't around as much."

"She's been living out her dream. I couldn't be happier for her. I love Jax, and he makes her happy."

Again, not a lie. I miss her like hell, but it's not like we're connected at the hip. She's always had her life, and I've had mine. Jax is perfect for her, even if he has her turning into a world-class traveler.

"What's going on with this Finn?"

Gah, I should've known he'd find a way to bring him up. I mentally kick myself for not seeing this sooner.

Rolling my eyes, I sigh heavily. "Dad, you know I don't do serious relationships." Yeah, I'm sure that's just what every dad wants to hear... not.

Before he can respond, I quickly point out, "Finn and I have only been out on a couple of dates." Technically, again not a lie. "Please don't make it out to be anything more than that. I need to be focusing on building my career, not getting serious with anyone."

"I swear I had this same conversation with each of your sisters... and look where *that's* got them?" Grumbling, he shakes his head. "Two future sons-in-law in two years... that's where it got me." In a high-pitched mocking tone, he adds, "*I'm focusing on my career.*" Just like my sisters would have said to him. I almost laugh at his ridiculous tone... but know better.

"I swear... life was so much simpler when the four of you only wanted to play dress up and make-believe games with me, and I was the only prince you needed. Now, half of you are engaged... one of you getting married *this week*... and another... well, it's only a matter of time." Returning his attention to me, he places a hand on mine. "You... well...You've always kept guys at bay... but..."

"Daaaad..." I cut him off, not liking where this is going. "I'm young and enjoying my life. I'm not ready for anything serious, and I don't see that changing anytime soon." I wish I could just tell him the truth and ease his mind. That things between Finn and me have an end date, and he has nothing to worry about. But that would defeat the purpose of our entire arrangement.

With a pleading look, he asks, "Will you at least tell me when someone special comes into your life, so I know I should take things more seriously? I've never had to worry much about you, but I'm not ready to be blindsided either."

On a heavy exhale, I squeeze his hand. "Trust me, Dad... if someone suddenly becomes important, it'll blindside me, too. But I won't need *you* to run them off; I'm capable of doing that all on my own."

"Raven," he warns, clearly not liking my negativity. "You can't cut yourself short."

"First, you don't want me to date anyone seriously, and now you do. You're like a yo-yo here, Dad. Make up your mind... wait... scratch that. Let's just let me be young and have fun and *not* try making things more than they are. Deal?"

Shoulder checking me with a grin, he chuckles. "Deal."

Chapter 10
Raven

"Ohmigod," Sloane cries out as tears form in her eyes. "Lanie, you look so beautiful. That dress is utter perfection. The way it fits you like a glove, and those details in the lace with the intricate beading is absolutely stunning!"

"Ryan's gonna lose his mind," I tease truthfully. "Though that poor man also gets gooey-eyed when you're wearing mismatched pajamas and your hair looks like a haystack. You could show up in a sack dress, and he'd think you're the most perfect person on the planet. But this dress... well, it's beyond words... it's... it's... impeccable!"

Lanie gazes at herself in the full-length mirror, taking in the details of her dress, twisting ever so slightly to see all the different angles. It's a white strapless lace ballgown, with a high-impact bodice that fits her like a second skin through her torso. The material itself is designed to shimmer in different lights, making her look even more radiant.

Twisting in my direction, she smiles. "Thanks. I knew this was the one the moment I tried it on. I couldn't believe it dropped perfectly to the floor without any alterations. There's no way I would've messed with all those details along the hem or at the waist. It would've ruined the design of the dress."

"Did you actually need any alterations?" Lizzy asks, looking Lanie up and down.

"Uh..." Lanie giggles as she looks to her chest. "I had to make sure the girls stayed contained. I was worried about it being strapless, and they put some sort of contraption into the boning of the dress... I think that's what they called it? I don't know. All I care about is I can dance the night away, and there won't be any wardrobe malfunctions."

The room fills with laughter. "Well... we wouldn't want that," Lizzy says as she steps in to hug Lanie. "Dad would have a coronary, and I'm sure Ryan wouldn't be far behind."

"I do wish Nana was here," Lanie says on a sigh. "Though I'm sure she played a part in this with her matchmaking skills. Without her attention to detail, Ryan and I would've never met."

Shaking her head, Sloane adds, "True. That woman always planned for everything... even after her death. Who the heck plans for a home renovation nearly a year later?"

"Nana," we all say as we burst into laughter.

"Well, you and your killer coat hanger must've done a number on Ryan because here you are, getting married on Saturday." I love the story of how they met. It will go down in history as epic.

"I think it had more to do with the fact she chewed him out in her undies than the coat hanger," Lizzy deadpans.

"Hey now," Lanie chides. "I thought the *Texas Chainsaw Massacre* was coming to get me. I had to do what it took to stay safe."

It's Sloane's turn to tease. She throws an arm around Lanie's waist and pulls her in for a side hug, and they make eye contact through the mirror. "Whatever makes you feel safe, Lane."

When the laughter dies down, Lanie turns to look at us. "I wish Mom's flight hadn't been delayed. I guess she'll have to wait until my big day to see this in person."

There's plenty of time for her to make it here before Saturday, but it's an added stress for everyone, nonetheless.

"Mom won't miss your big day," Sloane assures her. "Hell, I'm sure if she hadn't gotten a flight for tomorrow, she would've rented a car and driven all the way to Oregon."

Looking to each of us in our bridesmaid dresses, she smiles widely, effectively changing the subject. "I love these dresses on you."

"We do look pretty spectacular," I admit, turning to look at myself in the mirror.

Each of us have a deep burgundy dress that's the same shade, but in a style that fits our personality. I love that Lanie let us choose a dress we'd feel comfortable in and resemble each other, but not scream matchy-matchy. Maybe it's a twin thing but being dressed in the same exact clothes growing up is fun when you're six, not so much at nearly twenty-two.

Mine, for example, has a swoop over one shoulder, leaving the other bare, and crosses in the back, making me feel edgy, yet sophisticated at the same time. Sloane's is the traditional sleeveless with a V-neck bodice, while Lizzy's has the cutest halter that accents her tanned, toned shoulders perfectly. How each dress ties together from the way the bodice snuggly fits us, that leads to a sash tying at our waist and flowing into an A-line skirt, which drops to the floor. The dresses are like Lanie's, so they end right before our feet and don't drag on the ground. The difference between our dress and Lanie's is that they each have a slit up the side, that is not only functional, but makes me feel sexy as my leg peeks out of the silky material when I walk.

Stella, the shop owner, returns from helping another customer. "Is there anything you see needing changed or fixed?"

"No..." Lanie says, looking to each of us. "I think we're good."

"Great. Take your time. I'll get these dresses bagged up for you, and you can be on your way when you're ready."

At that moment, Lizzy's stomach rumbles. "Mind if we eat before digging into decorations?"

"Not at all. Let's grab some lunch at the Sea Breeze Café," Lanie suggests as Stella unbuttons her dress.

"Mmmm.... I need a bowl of their clam chowder," Sloane says from behind the curtain of a private dressing room. "I haven't had decent chowder since last summer."

The Sea Breeze Café is famous for their chowder. I'm convinced what makes it the best is the melted butter they put in before serving. "Thanks, Sloaney," I whine as my stomach growls in anticipation. "Now I'm craving that, too." Making us all laugh.

***

"IF MY CALCULATIONS ARE CORRECT, we need six more and we'll be done," Sloane says, counting the centerpieces in the middle of our kitchen table.

We're using pint-sized mason jars filled with fairy lights as a vase to put paper roses from Lanie's favorite books. Thanks to Ryan, when Sloane told him her plans, he helped out big time by reaching out to his best friend Vince. He pulled some strings to get us some copies of Charlotte Ann's books. Not only is Charlotte one of Lanie's favorite authors, she and Ryan met her on one of their first dates at a local book signing.

Apparently, it's a small world. Vince's twin sister, Vanessa, is married to Charlotte's brother. Now, thanks to these six degrees of separation, we're the proud owners of some of Charlotte's paperbacks, at very little cost to us.

"I absolutely love these roses," Lanie says, folding the paper

Sloane has precut, "but it still feels blasphemous... cutting up Charlotte's work."

"One, you already have a copy of this book," Sloane reminds her pointedly. "Besides that, the cover was damaged, and it's a book Charlotte couldn't sell. If it makes you feel any better, we only took apart this *one* book for the entire reception. Thanks to Charlotte's ability to write thick stories, many books were spared."

The front door swings open, and Mable's unique voice rumbles throughout the house as she singsongs, "Hello, Hello... Who's ready for some dinner?"

"We're in the kitchen," Lanie replies, keeping her focus on the flower.

Mable saunters into the room, and Dad and the guys follow her. Mable's renting a summer cottage a few streets away. She insisted on needing her downtime before the wedding and wouldn't hear of staying with us; she claimed she'd only be in the way. Apparently, she invited Mom to stay with her this week, so it's one less thing to worry about for everyone. She must've been cooking for a while because Dad, Ryan, and Jax all have containers with food in them.

"Mable, you didn't have to cook. We could've fixed something here," Sloane admonishes as she jumps to her feet to grab the dish from our aunt.

"Oh, nonsense, honey. I didn't. I may be old fashioned, but I've got my favorite restaurants here in town on speed dial. I ordered a chicken casserole from the diner down on Main Street. It came with all the fixins, including a berry cobbler for dessert. I had your dad pick me up, and he brought along the muscles." She points to the guys filing in the door. "To carry it all in the house."

Ryan enters the room, and his eyes find Lanie's in an

instant. "Hope you don't mind. I brought some help to finish decorations."

Lanie's vibrant smile lights up the room. "The more the merrier."

Ryan closes the distance between them and kisses her quickly before settling beside her.

Jax takes the seat beside Sloane, and I go back to focusing on folding and cutting the flower in my hand. I've just about got it right where I need it when I feel the hairs on the back of my neck tingle.

I look up to find Finn beside me, and my heart races. When his lips spread into a handsome smile, and he leans in to kiss me, it feels as natural as breathing.

"Hey," he says when he pulls back. "Need any help?"

Raising a brow, I challenge, "Any good at making paper roses?"

A low chuckle that only I can hear escapes. "Not even kinda. But if you tell me what to do, I'm sure I'll figure it out."

"I'll make you a deal; you hot glue, while I fold. It's a total pain in the rear, but it might go faster with your help."

"Put me to work; it's what I'm here for."

Oddly enough, Finn and I work remarkably well together. We fold, cut, and assemble the paper rose with ease, and before we know it, the entire vase is complete, and we're moving on to another one.

Eventually, Mable insists we eat before our food gets cold. Finn and I keep working until everyone has had a chance to dish up. When he reaches the counter before me, he effortlessly grabs a plate for each of us and dishes food onto my plate as we walk through the line. Then as if we are a real couple, he sets his plate next to mine at the kitchen table, kisses me on the cheek as if it's something he does every day, and wordlessly walks back to the fridge to grab each of us a Pepsi.

This man most certainly deserves an Oscar for acting the dutiful boyfriend.

Chapter 11
Finn

As soon as we finish eating, Raven and I manage to knock out these paper roses to finish off the decorations. It takes me a bit to get the hang of it, but as soon as we completed our first one, she led me through the process step by step, so we assembled two at a time.

"So, how did you get roped into this?" Raven asks diligently, folding the paper in front of her.

"Jax and I were hanging out at my new place when your dad called to see if he was coming to dinner. Once your dad found out where Jax was, he invited me to tag along."

"Who knew you'd be so good at this? Is there anything you can't do?" Jax interrupts. "Maybe Sloane and I can enlist your help with our wedding. I'm two left thumbs when it comes to crafting, and God only knows what this woman will come up with."

"Hey now," Raven turns to her sister and Jax, "Sloane will come up with something brilliant... But seriously, if you're using paper roses, we're recycling these. I don't even care if your favorite author isn't Charlotte Ann. I love you to the ends of the earth, Sloaney, but once is enough for assembling these."

"No kidding," Lizzy chimes in. "Do you even have a date set, Jax? Or are you just prepping us for the free labor?"

I don't miss the way Jax looks to Sloane for confirmation

before speaking. "We don't want to take away from Lanie and Ryan, but we've got something in the works."

"This is Sloane we're talking about," her father breaks in. "Of course, she's got a plan." Pointedly, he looks to his daughter. "Care to fill us in?"

"I truly don't want to take any light away from the two of you." She looks pleadingly at her sister and Ryan. "But with Ruby Frax going back on tour later this year, we'd like to be married sooner than later. Contrary to popular belief," she pauses and looks around the room, "I don't want a big wedding, and neither does Jax."

The reaction of her family is quite comical. Her dad stares wordlessly, and each of her sisters have a different version of their mouths hanging open in shock. Raven starts to speak, then stops herself and just stares at Sloane as if she's grown three heads.

"Oh, close your mouths," Mable admonishes. "Sloane knows what she wants and *hopefully,* she'll fill us in on it as soon as she's ready to let us know."

"Who are you and what have you done with Aunt Mable?" Raven asks. I have no idea if she's joking or not, but she's got the room's attention now.

"Thanks, Mable," Sloane says, holding onto Jax tighter. Looking to Lanie, she says, "We really don't want to disappoint you. Honest. We have no intention of taking attention away from your big day. But I won't lie about it to you either."

I feel Raven tense beside me, and the sudden tension can be cut with a knife as Sloane takes a long look at each of her other sisters, then her dad, before returning to Lanie. "Jax and I have been talking about this a lot... and with everyone already in town... and Jax's family living here... we've thought about a small beach ceremony with only immediate family and close friends. Please don't get me wrong... I've absolutely loved helping you plan your wedding, but all I need at mine is Jax and our family. The paparazzi's attention is already insane with Jax and his new band. So... *if* we were to plan anything, it could turn into utter chaos."

Jax stuns us all when he says, "We don't want a big ceremony or to interfere with anything. In fact, we'd prefer none of this even gets out publicly until after it's over. So, to answer your question, we'd like to get married a few days after yours before you leave for your honeymoon." Pointing to the ocean behind us, he adds, "We just want a simple ceremony out there on the beach."

Looking to Lanie, Sloane pleads with tears in her eyes. "Are you mad at me?"

Slowly, she shakes her head. "Why would I be mad? We all love Jax, and you're getting married. This is a big day for you." Then her eyes narrow as she asks, "If we hadn't directly confronted you, would you have even told us before our wedding?"

Sloane just stares at her sister, as Jax clears his throat. "The plan was to tell you all after your ceremony. We have no intentions of interrupting your big day."

"You haven't," Lanie assures her as she reaches across the table and squeezes Sloane's hand.

"Leave it to Sloane... planning something like this," their dad grumbles, effortlessly breaking the tension in the room, causing us all to laugh. "It's a good thing I took a few weeks off for leave. Now I've got *two girls getting married this week.*"

"Oh, she's got things planned." Jax chuckles. "Trust me."

Conversations around the room continue, but my attention is drawn to Raven and her sister when I notice Raven tilt her head at Sloane and stare expectantly. I swear an unspoken conversation passes between them, and I'd give anything to know what's being said. The moment passes quickly when Sloane breaks the silence as she looks between her sisters.

"I'd really like the three of you to be in the wedding party, like we've planned forever. Raven, you'll still be my maid of honor, right?"

Each sister agrees in their own way, but my attention stays on Raven, whose eyes shimmer with unshed tears. Reaching under the table, I squeeze her hand to let her know I'm here for her.

"Of course, I will, Sloaney. You know I wouldn't miss it for the world."

"Do you have a dress picked out?" Mable interrupts, drawing my attention to her. "Or do we need to see if Stella can rush you something?"

Sloane shrugs almost impishly. "Yeah. I found one... and I may have picked out some for each of you as well... I'll show you all tomorrow once Mom arrives."

"Hopefully, her flight won't be delayed. I know she's got to be beside herself for missing Lanie's fitting today," Mable adds as she walks to the island to dish up cobbler. "Anyone want ice cream with their dessert?"

"Here, let me help you with that," Mr. Lancaster says to Mable as he joins her in the kitchen.

Conversations start around the room as dessert is passed out. Most are digging in, but Raven's just staring at her bowl, pushing the fruit around. She hasn't joined any of the conversations around her and is clearly stuck in her head.

This isn't like her. Something's definitely off.

Maybe she needs a break?

Not wanting to call her out on it publicly, I whisper so only she can hear, "Hey, wanna take this outside?"

Startled, she looks from her dessert to me and shrugs.

"Come on," I say, standing, then taking her bowl in my hand. "I could use some fresh air. Mind if we finish this on the deck?"

I don't look around the room. Instead, I focus on balancing her bowl on my forearm so I can still hold mine and reach for her with my free hand. Thankfully, she takes it and follows me out the sliding glass doors with ease.

Once we're alone and sitting on the rocking swing that faces the ocean, I hand her back her dessert. She whispers, "Thanks."

Never being one to avoid a problem, I look her over with care and ask, "Everything okay?"

"Yeah." She blinks a few times. "Why wouldn't it be?"

"I don't know. You tell me. You've been stuck in your head since your sister dropped that bomb in there."

She lets out a sound like a cross between a snort and a harumph. "Just trying to take it all in. It's a lot to process. I couldn't be happier for Sloane and Jax, but I never expected she'd want to get married so soon."

"It's a rather short engagement, but I get why they're doing it."

Raven's brows scrunch together adorably, as she asks, "You do?"

"I was with them in close quarters while on tour. They're madly in love and when we go back on tour later this year, I'm sure their life will only get crazier. If they want to take a moment for themselves and share it with your family while they're home, I don't blame them."

Sighing heavily, Raven smiles weakly. "Don't get me wrong. I'm so happy for them. I love my sister, and Jax is the best. It's just a lot of... change."

Wrapping an arm around her, I pull her into my side. On her next heavy breath, she sinks into my chest, and I feel her relax into me. Neither of us says anything as she takes a few bites of her dessert, and we stare out into the waves in the distance. Eventually, she breaks the silence by tilting her head so she can look me directly in the eye and ask, "How did you know I needed this break?"

There are so many ways I can answer this question. Knowing she's strong-willed, stubborn, and could read a lot into each answer, I go with the most direct response. "It's simple. I paid attention."

Before she can think too much about that, I do the one thing I've been dying to do since arriving at the house. I lean in and kiss her gently.

The moment she melts into me, it's as if everything suddenly feels right again.

Chapter 12
Finn

Jax and I are meeting Ryker at the studio this afternoon, but he calls and asks if I'd grab lunch with him first. Knowing how much it takes out of me to finish a song, I eagerly agree.

He chooses a restaurant on the edge of town with the best French dip sandwiches, or so he says. Once we settle into the booth with our food, he stares at me instead of digging in right away, which is odd. This man always has an appetite.

"Something on your mind?" I ask after taking my first bite.

"You and I've gotten close this last year on tour. In fact, you've become one of my best friends. I don't want to make this weird, so I'll come straight out with it. Will you be my best man?"

I'm not sure what my expression shows, but I wasn't expecting this.

Before I can respond, Jax continues, "You've become important to both Sloane and me on tour. We couldn't imagine not having you included in our special day."

Clearing my throat, I quickly say, "Uh, yeah. Of course. I'd be honored."

Jax's grin is infectious. "Great. I'm gonna ask Ryker and Ryan to be my other groomsmen."

"Do I need a tux?"

Thankfully, Jax shakes his head. "No. We're not wearing

them. Apparently, Sloane only needs to know your sizes, and she'll take care of everything. We're going for a casual beach wedding, where we'll wear white shirts and dress pants."

"Really? I thought she'd want something more formal. With Sloane being the epitome of being a planner."

"I know, right?" Jax laughs. "But I think with all the planning for Lanie and Ryan's wedding, she wants to keep it simple and fun, with very little stress for everyone involved." Then he shakes his head. "If you think she's not planning everything to a T, you clearly don't know my future wife... Huh... wife... I love the sound of that." Jax's expression turns gooey, and I swear the man has stars twinkling in his eyes.

"She's perfect for you." I grin at seeing how smitten he is with her. Then I admit, "I hope one day I'm as lucky as you are to find someone so special."

Why the hell does Raven's beautiful face pop into my brain at this moment?

Surely, it's because we're talking about Sloane, and they're identical twins.

That's gotta be it, right?

No, dumbass, you're clearly thinking of Raven. Let's face it, you've hardly stopped thinking of her since the day you met... and now, you're stuck pretending to be her boyfriend during some of the biggest moments of her family's lives.

Fuck, will they all hate me when things between Raven and I end?

Clueless to my internal freakout, he grins widely. "I really hope that for you, man. It's the best feeling in the world."

I'm sure it is. Maybe someday I'll experience it.

"As the best man, are there any other responsibilities I should know about? What about a bachelor party... a speech? You know I'm down to help with anything you need."

"Ah... we're all going out for beers on Wednesday for Ryan.

I'm good with that." He's quiet for a moment as he finally takes a bite of his sandwich. When he's done chewing, he chuckles once. "Ha... I'm probably the least rockstar-like-groom on the planet. All I want is to make music and spend my time with Sloane. I could give two shits about anything else."

"That kind of attitude will keep you successful at both," I encourage. I've seen plenty of people in this business lose focus on their priorities, leading them on the shortcut to disaster. Jax, well, he's the real deal. He loves music, but if he chose to walk away from it, I'm positive he'd land on his feet.

"That sure is the plan. I love her, and I'm thrilled her family is on board with our impromptu wedding." Taking a sip of his soda, he chuckles. "Hell... I half-expected her dad or someone in her family to ask if she were pregnant... She isn't, for the record... But I wouldn't blame them for asking."

"Y'all had a valid reason to keep things on the down low. The moment you step back on stage at the Seaside festival, and we release our first single as a band, you're gonna be back in the spotlight for the foreseeable future."

"Uggg... don't get me wrong. I want to make it big with our band. But I won't deny I loved my low-key life in Seaside. Sure, I get recognized by locals, but they knew me before fame, so they don't treat me much different from before. Besides, it's such a tourist town, I can still stay on the fringe of being recognized."

"This new album we're working on hopefully will change that for all of us."

Lifting his glass to mine, he clinks it. "Here's to the success of Ruby Frax!"

"Hear-hear," I agree, taking a drink. Then return to my sandwich.

Damn. This is delicious. Before I know it, I've eaten the entire first half of the French dip and a good majority of my fries. There's something so good about dipping the crinkle fries into the house fry sauce that I can't get enough of.

Jax's phone buzzes on the table.

Immediately, I know it must be from Sloane, if the goofy grin on his face says anything. When he looks up, he asks, "You in for a bonfire with the Lancasters tonight?"

"I... uh... haven't really been invited," I admit.

Rolling his eyes, he types something into his phone, then looks to me. "This is me inviting you."

"But Raven..." I start, however Jax quickly interrupts.

"Please don't take this the wrong way. But as one of my closest friends, there's something you need to know."

Chewing on his lower lip, he waits until he has my full attention.

The longer he stares, the faster my heart rate increases. Fuck, does he know our entire relationship is a farce? Does he know something about her I don't?

When his silence nearly kills me, I prod him along. "Out with it, Jax. I'm sure there's not much you can say that I don't already know." Well, there is, but nothing I'd be surprised over if I'm being honest.

"Again... this has nothing to do with you," he assures me. "But... geez, how do I say this? Well... Raven... she... uh... doesn't let a lot of people in. She's more of a short timer when it comes to relationships."

"Okay..." I draw out, wondering where he's going with this.

"Well, the two of you... your paths are gonna cross frequently. I'd just hate to see you hurt."

"Wait, you're more concerned that she's gonna break my heart? Shouldn't your warning be the other way around, given that you're marrying her sister?" I ask defensively, though who I'm defending at this point is still up in the air. I know he's only trying to warn me, but I don't like him talking shit about her either.

Oh, what a tangled web we weave...

"Man, I've seen the way you look at her when you think no one's watching. You like her."

"So what if I do?" There's no point in denying it. If he's got an in with her, maybe he'll help me convince her to eliminate the *fake* part of this relationship.

"Raven... well... she's been known to keep guys at bay. She's not a player... more of a serial monogamist... but she doesn't let guys get too close."

Cocking my head to the side, I scrutinize his expression as I ask, "Why are you telling me this?"

"Well..." Jax takes a moment to consider his words. "One, you're my friend. Now that we've formed Ruby Frax, you're gonna be around. It's evident you like her, and I don't want to see either of you hurt. But *two*... if I'm right... I think she likes you, too. But she won't admit it."

What the fuck? Are we in middle school?

Why the hell does this bit of information suddenly give me hope?

Should I break her confidence and just tell him about our arrangement, or do I get his take on getting her to consider more? I really like Raven and even though we had an explosive start, I know it goes far beyond a physical connection.

That last thing he said though... I need to know more.

"What makes you so sure she likes me?"

Jax suddenly looks as if he's sucked on a lemon; his face scrunches and almost looks pained. "Please don't take this the wrong way, but you're spending time with her *outside* of a bedroom. You're more than just a physical connection for her."

Rage infuriates me. Instantly, I come to her defense. "Do you really think that little of Raven?"

Now it's his turn to backpedal. "God, no. I love her to the ends of the earth. But she's been known among her sisters for being open to sex-only situationships. She's not promiscuous, and exclusive while they're together, but she doesn't stick with any guy long-term. And before you say anything—" he cuts me off.

"There's absolutely nothing wrong with that. Trust me, I don't have any double standards when it comes to men and women enjoying each other and playing the field. You're all single and what you do is your business—no judgement here."

"What is your point?" I grind out through gritted teeth. My patience is running thin, and he's skating on very thin ice when it comes to my tolerance for talking about Raven's sex life. He's right. It's none of his business.

"Look, man..." His tone softens. "Next week, I'm marrying Sloane. She's not only her twin sister but her best friend. Sloane knows Raven better than anyone. But she also worries that Raven will never open herself up to love. She has no idea what her hangups are but as one of *my best friends*, I don't want to see you get in too deep, only to have her cut you loose, if you know what I mean. Raven's a bolter... and I... well, I guess this is my way of giving you fair warning."

"Any suggestions on changing that for her?" flies out of my mouth before I realize what I'm asking. What the fuck? We're supposed to be fake dating. I wait on bated breath as he ponders my question, not knowing why his answer suddenly matters so much.

"I know you're good with casual. Hell, you're a musician who travels all over the world. We're known for being the kings of casual. *But* if things are going in the different direction, like I think they are, if I wanted more with her, I'd keep showing up. Keep making her laugh. Keep making her see there's no reason to run when things get real. Hell, show her things *are* real. I don't think anyone's ever done that, according to Sloane. Raven always finds one excuse or another to keep guys at bay. I personally like you for her and hope things work out."

Thoughts twist through my mind like a tornado. Is what we have just casual? Do I even want more with Raven? This isn't supposed to be serious. Hell, we are FAKE DATING, I practically scream at myself. But why does the thought of losing her make me feel as if my insides are being ripped out by a bulldozer?

Chapter 13
Raven

I'm sitting on a blanket in the sand at the bonfire with my family, roasting a marshmallow, when my body tingles with a sense of awareness. When I look toward the house, my heart thuds in my chest when I spot Finn and Jax approaching with drinks in each of their hands.

I knew it was a possibility that Finn would show tonight, but I wasn't certain. I should've been the one to reach out since this isn't a public appearance and only involves my family, but I wasn't sure if I should ask him. So, I chickened out and let it go.

Gah, I'm being stupid. He's one of Jax's best friends.

Of course, I should've invited him. But I've been busy catching up with Mom, trying on dresses for a second wedding this week, and doing a freelance job for Smashing Waves Records. Time sort of slipped away today.

Not wanting to burn my marshmallow, I focus my attention on the flames in front of me, while I wait for them to join us. My eyes may be on the embers, but my head is solely focused on Finn.

Even from here, I can tell he looks exceptionally hot today. He's wearing what I joke with myself as his rocker uniform. His black jeans, boots, and a hoodie make him look like a tasty treat I want to lick all over.

"Raven, are you okay?" Mom asks, breaking me out of my fantasy.

"Yeah, Mom. I'm good."

"Oh..." She claps excitedly. "I see Jax and Finn are here. Is Ryker coming, too?"

"You know them?" I ask dumbfoundedly.

"Oh, yes. We met for dinner after I caught one of their shows outside of Richmond, Virginia. I love their music. I can't wait to see them play officially as Ruby Frax."

"I have yet to hear them live," I admit. Though I can't wait to watch them at the Seaside Music Festival in a few weeks.

"You're in for a treat when you do." Mom stands from her chair and hugs Jax when he approaches. "Congratulations, honey. I'm so happy for you and Sloane. I love you both so much." Then as soon as she releases him, she turns to Finn and squeezes him tightly. "I'm happy to see you, too, Finn."

"It's great to see you again, Ms. Lancaster," Finn says as she releases him.

"Oh, nonsense, call me Sarah. Please." Then she points an accusing finger at Jax. "You, too, mister. We'll be family in a matter of days, and I won't hear of such formalities."

"Okay. Okay." Jax laughs. "I'll call you Sarah. Sorry I wasn't here when you arrived, but we had some time booked in the studio for our new album."

"I can't wait until I can listen for myself. I'm a huge fan of Jax Cartwright on his own." She hip bumps him then adds, "Though I can't wait to officially hear Ruby Frax."

"Mom," I admonish. "Let them sit and relax. They've been working all day and could use a break."

Jax says something to her, but my attention is on Finn when he turns to me and asks, "Want a soda? Your dad and Mable said they'll be out soon with more snacks."

I smile, reaching for the Pepsi in his hand. "Thanks. I'm glad you could make it. I'm surprised Ryker isn't with you."

Finn shrugs as he settles on the blanket beside me. "He had other plans. Did the dress shopping go well?"

Rolling my eyes, I recall the events of the day, "You could say that. Sloane already picked out the dresses and had our sizes thanks to our last fittings with Lanie. We literally only had to show up to see if they fit. I've got your outfit hanging in my room if you want to try it on later."

"Seriously? She already has our clothes, too?"

Clearly, he's underestimated my sister.

"Did you forget we're dealing with Sloane here? She probably had these picked out two seconds after Jax proposed. That girl's a planner."

"Yeah. I should've known better. I spent months with her on tour." He chortles as he reaches for the graham cracker and chocolate I have placed beside me. Holding them out, he asks, "You ready for these?"

"Yes, please."

Pulling my stick back, I let him slide the golden-brown marshmallow off with the graham cracker and chocolate. Once they're off, he trades the stick in my hand for the s'more in his. "Here you go, sweetness."

Leaning in, he kisses my cheek before handing over the s'more. I'm not sure if he's doing it for the crowd, or if that's how he genuinely meant to greet me. My pulse picks up, and I find myself leaning into him for much longer than necessary. His lips feel warm against my cool skin, and I savor the smell of his cologne before he pulls away.

"Thanks," I mutter, though I'm not entirely sure what I'm thanking him for, as my brain is currently in a Finn-induced fog.

"How was the rest of your day?" he asks as he places the marshmallow stick near the coals at the base of the fire.

"Honestly, it was busy. I got up early to do some designs for your record label. Then once Mom arrived, we've been on the go nonstop."

A gust of wind blows through, making me shiver. Finn must notice because he pulls me close, effectively blocking the wind. "There. Is that better?" he asks as I settle against him.

"Yeah, thanks. What about you? Did you get much done in the studio?"

"Yeah, we finished a song and made some great progress on another. Just a few more tweaks, and that'll be done as well. I think we've found another that we'll perform live for the festival."

"I can't wait to see it. Do you know what you're playing for Lanie's wedding?"

His arm squeezes me tight as he whispers in my ear, "I've been sworn to secrecy. You'll have to wait like everyone else to find out."

"Seriously?" I ask in disbelief. "It's not like I'm gonna tell anyone. Since when did Lanie get so secretive?"

"Since Sloane made us swear on our lives to keep the secret for Lanie. She's scary when she's mad, and I'm not about to cross her."

"I get it." I chuckle. But I'm usually never on the side where secrets are withheld. I'm not sure how I feel about this. "She's a force to be reckoned with. Well, to be fair... we all are when we're mad."

"Good to know. Hmmmm... I think this is just about done," he says as he pulls his delicious golden glob back from the fire. Within seconds, he has his own s'more assembled.

As he eats, we relax into one another, enjoying a casual

conversation about random things throughout our day. He tells me about a bridge that's giving them trouble, and I tell him Mable's antics of pointing out a guy Lizzy might be interested in. I'm so lost in Finn, I don't even notice Dad and Mable have arrived with the rest of my family out at the fire. It takes Jax breaking out his guitar to pull my attention away from the handsome man behind me.

It's an unspoken code that he'll only play cover songs, so he doesn't draw any unwanted attention from any passersby on the beach. He starts out with Ed Sheeran's "Thinking Out Loud" in honor of Lanie and Ryan, as that's their song. Then he moves onto "Wonderwall" by Oasis.

It gets interesting when Finn asks to borrow the guitar so Jax can take a break and eat the s'more Sloane cooked for him. At first, I thought he'd just play his favorites, but when he asks the crowd if there are any requests, Lizzy suggests "Our Song" by Taylor Swift.

Then we have our own version of karaoke, each of us taking turns to sing a song while Finn plays. When it gets to me, I decide to test his skills and ask for one of my favorites growing up. I'm certain he can't play "Lose Yourself" by Eminem. The next thing I know, I am standing in front of my family, belting out the words, channeling Marshall Mathers from one of my dad's favorite movies—*8 Mile*.

Somehow, I hit it hard and never miss a beat throughout the entire song. It's been forever since I've sung along to this, but I'll admit, I'm quite proud of myself for pulling it off.

The moment the song ends, Finn raises a brow and asks, "Can you sing this with me?"

Never being one to back down from a challenge, I simply nod and wait for the music. I love karaoke night and crush most songs.

When the beginning chords of "Shallow" by Lady Gaga

and Bradley Cooper play, relief floods through me. I know this song and should be able to keep up.

What I'm not prepared for is how moving Finn's voice is when he starts the opening lyrics. Sitting beside him, I'm in awe of how deep his words hit my soul. They take me to another universe where it's just the two of us singing to one another, rather than to the crowd around us.

I'm thankful he cues me in to my part because I am so lost in his eyes, I almost forget to join him. Taking a breath, I play my part and belt out Lady Gaga's first verse with all my heart. Having spent years in choir, I know I can carry a tune but locking eyes with Finn, I take this song to an entirely new level. Blocking everything out and just feel the music flowing between us. I sing through my solo verse, through the bridge, and into the chorus, harmonizing with Finn like I've never done before. When the song ends, I just stare at Finn until my family interrupts my trance with cheers, whistles, and catcalls.

Wide eyed, Finn mutters, "Did you feel that? It was fucking phenomenal."

All I can do is nod in agreement. I don't know what just happened, but the connection I felt toward Finn while singing was out of this world. I've never sung with such emotion before in my life.

"Well, I certainly won't be going next after *that* performance." Lizzy's voice carries over the crowd, causing everyone to laugh and officially bursting the bubble between Finn and me. I burst out laughing myself when she grumbles, "Living with freaking professionals... and I didn't even know it. How the heck do I even compete in this family? I thought karaoke would be fun... but apparently, the pressure's on."

Chapter 14
Finn

From the moment Raven and I finish our last note, I've been dying to get her alone. If her entire family hadn't been present, I probably would've kissed the living hell out of her. Our connection is so strong, I nearly forget they're even around until cheers erupt.

Somehow, I manage to keep playing a few more songs before Jax asks if he can play one of his favorites for Sloane. After an appropriate amount of time passes, I make up an excuse, needing to try on those clothes Sloane bought me before I need to take off.

Raven's hand slips into mine effortlessly, as we walk the dark path back to her house. The entire time, the electricity zips between us like a live wire I'm not sure I want to contain. I'm certain she feels the same by the way her strides pick up the closer we get to the house.

Once inside, she leads me to her room. Yes, the clothes I need to try on are in there, but I could truly give two fucks about them. Once the door clicks shut, she turns and launches herself into my arms, and all I care about is her.

My lips crash onto hers, and I finally free the beast that's been kept at bay since our first night together. Her arms wrap around my neck, and I lift her with ease to my full height.

Effortlessly, her legs wrap around my waist, and she kisses me with a sense of urgency, like never before.

Instead of traveling all the way to her bed, I merely turn and push her body against the wall. I need to touch her, to feel her, and make her mine in every way possible.

Her heated skin feels silky and smooth against mine, and the way she digs her nails through the stubble at the base of my neck drives me crazy with need. My hand tangles in her hair as I angle her perfectly and deepen our kiss.

It could be minutes, days, or months that we're completely consumed by one another. Every second that passes, the flames that flow between us ignite into an inferno I have no intention of extinguishing.

Eventually, we need air. Breaking apart, she pants as she looks at me with so much heat in her eyes, they might be turning into molten lava, making my heart melt.

Fuck, she's beautiful, and the need I feel reflected in her gaze makes me want her even more.

Breathlessly, she pants, "I know we have stipulations for this situation-ship... or whatever we're calling this... But would you be opposed to changing our terms... from hands-off to more like a friends with benefits for this fake dating we've agreed to? I really like you, and I'm tired of denying what we have between us."

Friends with benefits? Really? That's what she wants to call this?

Her words hit me like a pail of ice water, and I'm instantly brought back to my conversation with Jax. Clearly, Raven and I have a connection. I've known from the beginning I want more. But according to Jax, Raven doesn't do commitment and if I want to win her over like I think I can, I need to call her on her bluff.

As I pick my next words carefully, I let her body slowly

slide to the floor. Cupping her face in my palm, I wait until I've got her full attention before saying the words that will either gut me on the spot or make me the happiest man alive.

"What if I want more?"

Blinking rapidly, as if she doesn't comprehend my intentions, she asks, "More?"

"I want more," I repeat forcefully.

Disbelief still evident in her words, she clarifies, "More than friends with benefits? Or more than fake dating?"

"Yes," I state firmly. "To both."

"But... But..." she sputters as her long lashes blink rapidly. "We agreed... we had stipulations... there wouldn't be feelings involved."

Crossing my hands over my chest to keep from reaching for her, I remain as stoic as possible. "Things changed."

"What do you mean things changed? You said we'd be seen with each other in public, and you'd be my date to Lanie's wedding, well both weddings since Sloane and Jax sprang that on us."

"And I will," I assure her. "I'm a man of my word."

Tilting her head to the side, she studies my features. "Two seconds ago, you were ready to rip my clothes off and have your way with me. We were both on board with it. What changed?"

"My feelings," I admit honestly. "I really like you... for real. There's nothing fake about my feelings for you, and I refuse to pretend otherwise."

"But I wasn't looking for anything serious. I told you... from the start."

"I know, and at the time, neither was I."

For the longest time, she just stares at me, and it takes everything in me to remain rooted in place and not reach for her. These may be the hardest words I'll ever say, but my gut tells me by the look in her eyes that she has real feelings for me, too. She just might not be able to admit them aloud just yet.

When I can't take the silence any longer, I say, "Look, nothing has to be decided tonight. I know this is a lot for you to take in and now that you know where I stand, you can think about it and make the best decision for you."

"I... I... I don't know what to say." Her hands start to reach for me, and I almost step toward her, but I remain strong.

"Look, we still need to get through these next few weeks being seen together. Between your sisters' weddings and the festival, for both our sakes, we can't stop being seen together in public. You don't have to decide today. But please know I'll keep kissing you in public, holding your hand, and trying to win over your heart, but I can't go any further than that behind closed doors—unless you're willing to go all in."

"All in?" hangs on her lips, as her eyes widen with shock as she processes my words.

"All in," I assure her. "I want to date you for real, steal kisses when no one is looking, and get to know you on a deeper level. I won't pressure you or make you decide anything today. But I want you to know all deals are off when it comes to being in a fake situation-ship or whatever you called it. I like you, Raven Rene, and I'm willing to wait for you."

With that, I reach for the clothes hanging on the trim of her closet and walk out of the room, hoping like hell I didn't just make the biggest mistake of my life.

Chapter 15
Finn

The next few days are hell on earth. Raven and I have been at each other's sides through Lanie and Ryan's rehearsal dinner and wedding. Throughout the entire ceremony, I can't keep my eyes off Raven. She looks absolutely stunning as she walks down the aisle and stands beside her sisters. As I watch Lanie and Ryan declare their love for one another, I can't help but notice every time Raven glances my way, sparks fly between us.

I've been the dutiful date, being ever so attentive for the last few days. I greet her with a kiss on her cheek, escort her from room to room with a hand on her lower back, and hold her hand as we walk through town. It's pathetic how I've used nearly every excuse imaginable to touch her one way or another, but she doesn't seem to mind. In fact, sometimes, she reaches for me, even when no one is around to see.

I've made it my mission to win over her heart. I've seen firsthand how she's burning the candle at both ends, trying to start her new business and keep up with the needs of her sisters and their weddings. I've paid attention to the things she says and the little things she doesn't. As each day goes by, it's easier to read Raven, though she fights like hell to remain a mystery.

I've frozen my ass off by giving her my jacket during Lanie's rehearsal dinner, spent countless hours with her and her family, and have woken up at the ass-crack of dawn to bring her pastries from her favorite café in town that she can down with her morning cup of coffee. I'm doing my best to show her I'm serious about wanting more, by also giving her the space she claims to need, and not pressuring her for a decision anytime soon.

It's okay because I'm not going anywhere. Or at least that's what I keep telling myself. I'll jump over any hurdle she throws my way if she keeps looking at me with her playful smiles and longing stares when she thinks I'm not looking. To me, waiting for Raven to come around is worth it... even if it does feel like freaking forever at times.

We've agreed to keep whatever this is going between us through the festival because our original reasons for being seen together haven't gone away. Her walls may be high, but day by day, I see cracks in her armor, showing me this isn't all for nothing. She may not be ready to come out and say it, but her actions speak louder than her words.

As Ryan and Lanie say their vows, my attention is drawn to the adorable flower girl standing beside Lanie. When Jules notices Lizzy tearing up behind her, she reaches for her hand and squeezes it reassuringly. It's absolutely adorable.

Jules is the niece of Ryan's best friend from college. At the rehearsal dinner last night, we met Vince and his wife, Sydney, as well as his twin sister, Vanessa, and her husband Damien. Jules melted many hearts with her adorable wit and charm as she stole the show with her stories about being an expert flower girl. I nearly died laughing when Raven asked her if she was worried about being a flower girl. She stood proud and replied, "No. I've done this plenty of times. I've been one at Momma and Daddy's wedding, and for Unks and Aunt Sydney. Have *you* ever been in a wedding?"

"Nope," Raven had replied.

"Well, if you have any questions, I'm an expert at weddings. I'm sure I can help you."

With that, Jules ran off to her uncle Vince and asked for some dessert.

I'm brought out of my revelry about Jules when Jax starts singing "Thinking Out Loud." I'm sure everyone's eyes are suddenly on Jax as he performs; however, mine focus on Raven.

She looks absolutely breathtaking in her deep-burgundy dress. Her long hair is braided intricately into some sort of updo, making her neck and shoulders look sexy as hell. My heart skips a beat when Raven glances my way the moment Jax sings about people falling in love in mysterious ways. It picks up even faster when she gives me a knowing smile and a wink.

I've been falling for Raven more each day, but with that simple little smirk at the end, before she returns her attention to her sister and Ryan, I'm certain of one thing. I'm already gone, hook, line, and sinker.

I'm in love with Raven Rene Lancaster.

THE RECEPTION IS in full swing by the time I grab plates of food and drinks for Raven and me. She and the wedding party have been busy with greeting guests and taking a few more group photos with family and friends.

"Thanks. I'm starving," Raven admits when I settle in beside her.

"Need anything else?" I ask, knowing she's likely exhausted from the festivities of the day.

"Nope. I'm good. Hopefully, we'll get to eat this before the speeches and dancing." Looking at her sister Lanie, she adds, "I'm glad someone thought to put food in front of her. She was so nervous before the ceremony, she hardly ate today."

"I saw your mom dishing up plates as I went through the line. I'm sure she had something to do with it. By the way..." I draw out, waiting for her to look me in the eyes, "Since I clearly forgot to mention it earlier, you look absolutely stunning today. I can hardly keep my eyes off you."

"Finn..." She blushes as she bats a hand in my direction.

"A simple thank you will do," I tease. "No sense in getting bashful on me."

"Bashful is never a word I've had used to describe me," she guffaws and couldn't be more adorable.

"Well, take the compliment, and I won't have to use it again," I counter. "You're the most stunning woman in this room. No offense to Lanie—she's a beautiful bride. But you've captured my interest from the moment you walked in and haven't let go."

"Now you're just being delusional." She rolls her eyes, then dismisses my comment by taking a bite of the beef tenderloin on her plate.

Leaning in so that only she can hear, I challenge, "Do I need to prove it to you?"

Raven's eyes widen, but Sloane clinking her glass for the crowd's attention rescues her.

Once we're settled, Sloane says into the microphone, "Hi, for those who don't know me, I'm Sloane. I'm your emcee for the night. We're starting things off with a toast for the bride and groom. Vince, would you like to introduce yourself?"

Vince clears his throat and says, "Hello, everyone. I'm Vince Larson. I've had the privilege of knowing Ryan since our very first day of class at CRU. I guess you could say Ryan stood out. I mean, not many people are over a head taller than me."

The room fills with laughter, but he continues, "You see, I didn't know many people. I lived off campus with my sister and Jules, and my family was my priority. But from the moment

Ryan and I met, our friendship formed instantly. He may not know how much it meant that he was not only fun to hang out with, but he was kind and loving to my family and was there for us when we needed him most. Ryan quickly became the family we never knew we needed. It didn't hurt that he enjoyed Friday night game nights, which consisted of Chutes and Ladders with a toddler, rather than attending parties on campus. I'm sure it was because we offered him a home-cooked meal and got him out of his dorm room as often as we could."

Again, the room fills with laughter. While Vince waits for the crowd to settle, he looks to his wife Sydney. "The point I'm trying to make is after losing our parents, Ryan and, eventually, Lanie, became part of our self-made family. Throughout their last year of school, we've remained close to Ryan and fell just as much in love with Lanie as him. She's become an honorary aunt to Jules, and we couldn't be more grateful to have them in our lives." Looking around the room, he says, "Ryan and Lanie, I of all people know just how valuable and precious life is. A love like yours doesn't come around often, and I couldn't be happier to be here to celebrate the life you're building together. Everyone, please raise your glass to the bride and groom. May they grow old and gray together and fall more in love with each other each day."

Someone from the crowd shouts, "To the bride and groom!" And we all repeat it.

Before he hands off the microphone to Lizzy, the maid of honor, he asks Ryan and Lanie, "Do you mind if Jules says a few words? She saw me writing this speech and wanted to add a few thoughts of her own."

Ryan and Lanie both nod in agreement, and Jules steps up to the mic confidently. "Hi. I'm Julia Fallon, but everyone calls me Jules. I have a little advice that Momma once told me that I want to share with you. One, never go to bed mad. No matter how big your problems seem, they're easier when you work together to solve 'em. Two, for some reason, we're supposed to make our beds every day; apparently, that's what successful people do." The room roars with laughter when she shrugs and whispers away from the microphone. "I don't really know about that one." Bringing the mic back to her mouth, she says to the room, "My daddy Dame always tells me to love big with your whole heart and always try your best. I've never seen anyone love me or Momma as much as he does, so it must be good advice. Hopefully, it will work for you."

I hear Raven sniff, and her eyes are filled with unshed tears. After passing her a napkin, I reach for her hand and give it a squeeze, letting her know I'm here for her. Then I return my attention back to Jules.

"Last but not least, I wanna say thank you for letting me be a part of this. I love you, Ryan and Lanie. Congratulations!"

As the room fills with cheers, I look around. I see many dabbing at their eyes. That Jules just stole the heart of everyone in the room.

When Jules hands the mic over to Lizzy, she rushes over to hug both Ryan and Lanie before returning to her parents.

"Well... after that, I'm not sure what more I can say. I'm so honored to be here today to celebrate with my sister and her new husband Ryan. For those who might be confused, I'm Lizzy, the youngest Lancaster. I could go on and on about why I think Ryan and Lanie are perfect for each other, but if you've talked with either of them, you'd clearly see why. Instead of saying what I'd planned, I think you should remember Jules' speech. Love big, love hard, and I'll add don't forget—it's the two of you versus the problem when there is one; never one of you versus the other. I love you both 'till the end of time. Congratulations!" Lifting her glass, she adds, "To the bride and groom!"

Everyone finishes their food and after a while, Sloane returns to help cut their cake and announces the first dance. After that, the wedding party dances to their song, and I join Raven out on the floor. With her in my arms, all feels right in this world.

Now, if only I can convince her to stay.

Chapter 16
Raven

Right now, I feel as if my life is like that octopus ride I used to enjoy as a kid at the fair. Between my sisters getting married this week, I feel like I'm in constant motion. Up, down, spin around with all my might. There's a flow of synergy throughout my family, and I've never felt happier or more uncertain, especially when it comes to Finn.

My stomach flips and rolls with each move Finn makes in anticipation and dread for what's to come. I know our arranged time together is coming to an end. There's only a few more weeks until the festival, and then we'll likely go our separate ways.

But why does that make me feel like my insides are being ripped out with a rusty steak knife? I don't do serious relationships. I don't let guys as sexy, charming, and funny as Finn get close. I've purposely orchestrated my life so this never happens. It's why I keep things casual.

My mind replays my time with Finn at Lanie's wedding. We danced, we laughed, and we even shared the most amazing goodnight kiss imaginable, but when he turned, I let him walk away.

I'm not used to wanting more with a man.

Maybe that's why I'm up at the ass-crack of dawn, contemplating my life choices. I've never felt so frustrated and alone. I know my sisters and Dad are inside the house if I need them, but they're not who I want.

No, that would be the tall, tatted rockstar who's stolen my freaking heart.

I should grab my gear and go surfing. Maybe I can clear my head and figure out what I'm going to do about Finn. Running upstairs, I quickly change into my swimsuit and head out to the garage to grab my wet suit, booties, and surfboard. Just as I'm about to leave, Lizzy comes down and says, "Wait up. I'll go with you."

While I wait for my sister, I pack a few protein bars and a couple of bottles of our favorite sports drink for when we're finished. Not knowing how long we'll be gone, I also toss in a few bananas and some grapes into my sinch bag.

Our walk along the coast is quiet as we take in the morning air. I'm crap for company since I'm entirely in my head, but thankfully, she doesn't call me out on it. By the time Lizzy and I reach the cove, I'm crawling out of my skin with pent-up energy. I can't wait to get on the water. There are several others already out on dawn patrol with us, hoping to catch these early morning waves. After I stash my bag of treats in the rocks where the tide won't reach it, Lizzy and I make quick time of putting on our booties, pulling up our hoods, and running into the water with our boards.

Lizzy catches the first wave, and I watch her ride it until she glides closer to shore. As soon as I spot the right one for myself, I paddle with all my might and drop in perfectly. The moment I pop up on my board, all is right with the world again. It's nothing but me, my board, and this wave. Wash, rinse, and repeat. This is the perfect way to start my morning.

When my body is worn out, and I'm done with surfing for the day, I return to the rocks where I left our snacks. I'm ravenous and can't wait to give my body the nourishment it desperately needs. Plopping on the rounded rock, I grab a protein bar and lean against the rock behind me for support. Closing my eyes as I chew, I bask in the sun and listen to the ocean roar. Now that I'm not exerting energy, I'm feeling the effects of the fifty-five-degree water. Thankfully, we're on a bit of a heat wave, and the air is much warmer than the water as I wait for Lizzy, or I'd freeze.

"So, are you gonna tell me what's crawled up your butt? Or are we just gonna ignore it?" Lizzy asks, effectively breaking me out of my peaceful tranquility.

"What do you mean?" I ask, sitting forward. Now that she's placed her board next to mine, her hands punch into her hips and clearly, she's irritated about something.

"Well, you've barely said two sentences to me all day. You're hitting those waves harder than I've seen you try in years. You've taken some serious wipeouts today, and if I didn't know you better, I'd say you were almost punishing yourself or something. What gives, Raven?"

"First, I'm not punishing myself."

"You weren't takin' it easy," she counters. "We can go all day with you denying something's bothering you. If that's how you wanna play it, then fine. Orr..." she draws out. "You could just tell me what's going on. I know you're working through something. This is what you do. I get it. You're strong and independent. But being strong doesn't mean you have to go through *whatever this is* alone."

When I remain quiet for longer than she thinks I should, she huffs loudly, plops herself beside me on the rocks, and reaches for the drink I brought for her. Unscrewing the top, she takes several large gulps, then returns the lid before setting it beside her. Wordlessly, she reaches for a protein bar.

Maybe if I talk about my issues, she'll help me come up with something. Hell, I've spent nearly a week in my own head, and I've gotten no closer to finding an answer to what's plaguing me than before.

"Okay…" I exhale heavily. "But what we talk about needs to stay between us."

"Of course. But before you begin, can I ask, does this have anything to do with Finn?"

Blinking at her, I'm momentarily at a loss for words.

How the hell does she know?

When she keeps staring, I find my voice. "Why would you say that?"

"Oh, I don't know… you were caught coming out of his room by that idiot photographer. You've spent the last few weeks with him, and every time you think no one's looking, you're watching his every move. And don't even get me started on that performance at the bonfire. The two of you clearly have a connection."

"What? I have not," I protest, but damn, Lizzy's perceptive. Sometimes I forget that she may be younger than me, but she's clearly not so little anymore.

"You have. But that's not what's bothering you… so out with it."

"Ha… since when did you get all grown and knowledgeable?"

"Raven, I've been studying you my entire life. It's what little sisters do. Stop getting distracted and making me repeat myself. Does this have *anything* to do with Finn?"

In our family, we don't lie to one another. We might not tell each other every sordid detail, but when asked a point-blank question, we learned early on it's better to just speak the truth, deal with the problem, and then move on.

Shit. How do I even start?

"Yes… it has everything to do with Finn," I admit.

"Is he a closet jack hole or something? Do I need to kick his ass?"

That thought is almost comical.

"Ha... not even kinda. That's the problem. He's smart, funny, patient, and kind. He freaking gets me better than anyone outside our family. He makes me want for things I never imagined for myself."

"So... You like him..." she says, clearly amused. I can tell it's taking everything in her not to smile.

"Of course, I do!" I practically shout. "But I'm not supposed to. We agreed there was an expiration date. We had rules. We freaking started as a one-night stand. It was supposed to stay casual and fun, not turn into *this*!"

"Define the *this*, you're clearly unhappy with."

"I was supposed to act like his girlfriend... not freaking catch feelings for Finn!" I practically shout exasperatedly.

Narrowing her eyes, she purses her lips. "Act like his girlfriend?"

"Yes, act. It was the easiest way to clear his and Sloane's names, *and* it got Mable off my back. It was a win-win and fail proof. I thought I could have a little fun this summer, and then we'd go merrily on our way... separately of course."

"And now you don't want that?"

"God, don't you see? That's the crux of this entire problem." I stand and pace in front of her.

"What do you mean?"

"I mean this was supposed to be casual. Not only did *I* freaking catch feelings, but he has the audacity to want more."

"So..." she draws out slowly as if she's choosing her next words carefully.

Good... because I'm losing my shit, *and she should* be careful.

"You don't want more?"

To make my point, I spit out each word as its own sentence. "Liz. I. Don't. Do. Relationships."

"You might not have in the past, but what's wrong with being with Finn now?"

Gah, she has the gall to be rational.

"Well, for starters... he's not only one of Jax's best friends, but he's in Ruby Frax and will forever be connected to our family. What happens when things go wrong?"

"But what if they go right?" she quickly counters, clearly channeling Nana as that was one of her favorite sayings.

"I could fuck up everything for our entire family if things go sideways. That's just too much risk."

"Look, it's getting late, and I need to get ready for work. So please think about this... you don't have to decide anything right now. Take that pressure off yourself. It's not helping, and you'll know the answer to my next question when you're ready."

"Okay... this has gotta be good," I mutter to myself.

But she ignores my jab. "I do want you to seriously think about this. One day, Finn will move on. He'll find someone who loves him like he deserves. You said it yourself. He'll forever be connected to our family. My question for you is... how are you gonna feel if it isn't you?"

Chapter 17
Finn

My eyes keep drifting to Raven throughout the entire ceremony. She's taken my breath away since making her appearance today for pictures. She's wearing a cornflower-blue dress, or so she called, that accentuates her every curve and falls just below her knees. It's like her sisters, as they're all the same shade, but each bridesmaid has it styled uniquely. Raven tried to explain that these dresses were versatile, as they could be styled in over one hundred different ways, but I'll have to take her word for it. I could truly care less. All that matters to me is how radiant she is as she peeks at me while Jax and Sloane say their vows.

While words are spoken about loving one another completely, her eyes shimmer with unshed tears, and her smile grows. When her eyes meet mine, her cheeks turn the most beautiful shade of pink, then she blinks rapidly and looks away. Sometimes her expression turns serious, and I'd give just about anything to know what's going on in that brilliant brain of hers.

Has she given what I said any more thought? Is she considering more with me? Or have I lost my chance by keeping her at bay?

My heart aches at just the thought. Instinctually, I know I'm doing the right thing, but it's harder than I imagined waiting for a response. I've been on pins and needles since laying my feelings out there. Patience is a virtue that's running thin and if she doesn't make up her mind soon, I may have to switch up my antics.

Suddenly, the crowd erupts in cheers, and I frantically look around to see what's happening. Jax and Sloane are just pulling back from their kiss, and the music starts as they walk down the makeshift aisle in the sand.

How did I miss the entire ceremony?

Looking to Raven, I hold out an elbow for her to use as I escort her down the aisle behind the bride and groom. Feeling her squeeze my arm in excitement has me picking up my pace, eager to spend more time with her. The way her fingers graze my skin makes my body hum in anticipation.

Sloane and Jax opted to forgo a formal reception. Instead, they have hired a caterer and plan to have a barbeque at their family's home after the ceremony. They assured Mable, when she asked, that they would still uphold all the traditions but on a smaller scale. I, for one, can't wait to get Raven on the dance floor, so I have a reason to keep her in my arms. If I had my way, I wouldn't let her go all night.

Once we've walked down the aisle, I'm forced to release Raven as she rushes to Sloane and hugs her fiercely. "I'm so happy for you, Sloaney." Then she hugs Jax just as tight. "I love you, too, Jax. Let me be the first to officially welcome you to the family."

Before either can say more, the bride and groom are rushed with an onslaught of people, all giving their best wishes. As I awkwardly stand and watch, Raven steps up beside me and reaches for my hand. Her other hand snakes around my arm, and she squeezes me tight. "God, I'm so happy for them."

"So am I," I agree. "This moment is magical."

While we wait for the after party, or so they're calling it, Raven and I mingle with the rest of the wedding party and her family. Before we know it, the bride and groom have returned and food is served as music plays quietly in the background. They've hired a deejay to mix music and play the part of emcee, as Jax was insistent Ruby Frax should enjoy the night with their family and loved ones, not perform for everyone.

From one event to the next, my focus remains on Raven. I barely remember the words to the speech I've given once she steps up to give hers.

Taking the mic firmly in her hands, Raven slays it with her speech. "Jax, I've had the honor of living with Sloane since being roommates in the womb. She's more than my sister; she's my best friend. When she met you, I knew you were the one for her. Heck, I knew it before either of you could pull your heads out of your asses and realize it for yourselves. I know your love is special and pure. I'm expecting you both to love, honor, and cherish each other until forever. I wish you the best and will love you both until the end of time. Congratulations! Please lift your glasses to the bride and groom!"

After our speeches, Sloane and her father dance, and then they ask the wedding party to join them on the deck. Wrapping Raven in my arms, we glide across the floor. When I'm here with her like this, I've never felt so right.

We continue dancing for a few more songs, until Raven sighs heavily and asks, "Would you mind taking a walk with me? I could really use a break."

Without another word, we slip out of the crowd and quickly make our way to the promenade. Raven's quiet as we walk and the sounds of the party behind us slowly disappear. Once the sound of the ocean is all we hear, Raven pulls us to a bench where we can sit and watch the waves crash onto shore.

"Everything okay?" I ask when I can't take the silence any longer. Obviously, she's got something on her mind, and she might as well tell me so we can handle this burden together.

"Yes and no." She shrugs.

A panicky feeling shoots through my body, and I'm immediately on edge when she doesn't say more.

"Care to share?"

Sighing heavily, she leans into me as she intertwines our fingers and squeezes my palm. "I'm so happy for my sister. I truly adore Jax and wish them all the happiness in the world."

"That sounds like a good thing," I point out as I wait for the other shoe to drop.

My heartbeat pounds in my ears in such strong competition of the roaring ocean in front of us. I barely hear her say, "It's a very good thing."

"Then what's wrong?" I ask hesitantly.

"I never was the type who wanted the kind of love they have for each other."

This isn't where I thought our conversation would go. "What do you mean?" I ask cautiously.

"I've never had any intention of getting serious with anyone." She's said that before. So where is she going with this?

"But..." I draw out, then quickly ask the question I need answered, "why are you telling me this now?"

"You," she says, as if it explains everything so simply—though as far as I'm concerned, it's about as clear as mud.

"Me... what do I have to do with anything?"

"Everything." Again, the answer is simple in her mind and vague as fuck in mine.

"Before you, I was adamant that *I don't do relationships*," she emphasizes, and of course, my curiosity is piqued.

My heart thuds in my chest as I finally see where this conversation is going. "Is there a particular reason?"

"I kept people at a distance, so I wouldn't get hurt," she admits.

I can't imagine anyone not liking this beautiful woman. "How would they hurt you?"

"It's simple." She shrugs as she rubs her fingers up and down my arm. "They left."

"Who do you mean?" I know she lost her grandmother recently, but everyone else is still very much in her life.

"Since meeting you, I've done a lot of thinking. It hit me yesterday after Lizzy knocked some sense into me that I'm keeping you at bay because I'm afraid of losing you, too."

"You just barely got me. Do you think I'd be a fool to let you go so soon?" I counter, trying to get her to see that I have no intentions of going anywhere.

Then I process her words again. *Losing you, too.*

Hesitantly, I ask, "Just who else have you lost in your life?"

Shrugging, she whispers sadly, "Everyone."

"Okay, I'm completely lost. Please explain because I'm so confused."

"How do I put this so you'll understand? Hmmmm.... I guess what it boils down to is everyone I've come to love leaves me in one way or another."

Clearly, she's mistaken. This makes no sense.

Her heavy sigh has the muscles in my chest pulling tight and my shoulders tense. "Explain more, please."

"Okay, I swear. I'm not a drama queen having a pity party. But the reality is, every single person that I've grown to love has just up and left at one point in my life. It started with my dad. Being divorced from my mom early on was an adjustment for all of us. Then with him being in the military, he was often gone away on missions, making us miss our scheduled visitations with him for months on end. Even though Mom and Dad worked hard to keep us in one school district most of our lives, I had to make new friends often. With their parents being in the military, they only stayed for six months to maybe two years, if I was lucky, before their family was stationed some-where else. My friend group had a constant revolving door. I learned from an early age, not to count on anyone but my sisters, and I truly believed I didn't need anyone else if I had them."

My heart feels as if it's getting squeezed out of my chest as I patiently wait for her to finish this story. When tears form in her eyes, the organ beating behind my ribs may as well be ripped to shreds.

Wiping her eyes, she takes a steadying breath before continuing, "Then Lanie went off to college, Sloane and I grad-uated high school, and even Mom left to become a traveling nurse." This causes a tear to spill over and leak down Raven's beautiful face, and I finally think I see where this is going.

I start to say so, but she just squeezes my hand and practi-cally begs, "Please let me finish. I've never told anyone my reasons to remain independent and most importantly, single."

Wiping at a tear from her eye, I feel her body relax, and she traces the ink of my tattoos. "You see... from the time we were born, it was Sloane and me against the world. Don't get me wrong, I'm close with Lanie and couldn't imagine my life without Liz, but Sloane was my everything. In fact, up until last year, we did everything together. School, summer camp, our first jobs, even college. You name it—we were inseparable."

"And then she went on tour with Jax," I break in, finally putting the pieces together. Oh my fucking God, this woman has literally had everyone she cares about walk away one way or another. No wonder she keeps everyone at bay.

Without knowing my epiphany, she insists, "I would *never* begrudge Sloane for having a life of her own. I'm truly happy for her, but yes, it hurt like hell watching her go. But I would do it again in a heartbeat to see a smile like she's wearing today for just five minutes. She's so happy with Jax... and I feel like a petty bitch for missing her as much as I do. When she went away, it was like a part of me went missing, too."

Fuck, she's so strong and brave. And to think she's kept this to herself all these years. I hope like hell that by her telling me this, she's considering letting me in to that fortress she resides in. If I get that honor, I will do my damnedest to be the man she deserves.

"You said this had something to do with me?" I ask hesitantly. "If you haven't figured it out, I'm not going anywhere—no matter how much you try pushing me away," I pointedly remind her.

"This has everything to do with you, Finn, because I blame you for making me feel. You big jerk, you've made me want more, and I can't force myself to walk away before you have the chance to hurt me."

Wrapping my arms around her, I pull her close. "Raven, I have no intention of walking away. I'm a fucking fool in love and can't imagine my life without you. If I have to prove to you that I'm not going anywhere, I will."

This has Raven's eyes snapping toward me in a nanosecond.

"You love me? As in you really love me? But we just met. How can that be?"

"For the love of all that's holy," I mutter under my breath. "Why on earth can't you believe that I've fallen for you? I wake up thinking of you and dream about you every night when I'm asleep. You consume all my freaking thoughts. So much so, I even wrote a freaking song—about you—and had to lie to the guys so I wouldn't give my feelings about you away. Because I'm a freaking man of my word, and I was the idiot who promised to keep things between us."

"Well, fuck that shit." I shake my head, annoyed with that hard truth. "I'm not keeping my feelings about you to myself any longer. I love you, Raven, and I want everyone to know about it. If you don't like that side of me, well, sweetness, you're gonna need to get used to it!"

"It may have taken me forever and a day to realize it... but fucking hell... I love you, too, Finn McGowen. You made me break every rule I've ever had. So, what are we gonna do about it now?"

I don't even think.

My lips are on hers the moment I process her words. She tastes of everything I've been missing in my life. She feels better than that first drop of rain after an immeasurable drought. The way her sexy moans escape, I need to take her home and show her just how much she means to me.

Chapter 18
Raven

I hope my sister will forgive me, but Finn and I won't be returning to her wedding. The moment I shared my past, a weight was lifted. I could finally see clear for the first time in forever. I'm fucking in love with Finn McGowen. I love him with my whole heart, and there's not one single thing in this world stopping us from being together.

By the time we get back to the cottage he's renting, our energy is more combustible than our first time together. My desire for him is no longer just scratching an itch or having a good time. My need is carnal and beyond anything I've ever experienced. My heart feels like it might burst out of my chest, knowing his need matches mine.

He loves me.

Finn fucking loves me.

How did I not see this earlier?

For weeks, he's shown me with his actions, but to hear the words with my whole heart open to being loved takes everything to an entirely new level. Finn feels like he was made for me. Like he somehow gets me on a deeper level than Sloane, if that's even possible. I know without a doubt he'll never seek to replace her. He simply needs to share his life with me and make me his in every way.

Within seconds of entering his bedroom, our clothes are strewn across the floor as we fervently kiss our way to his bed. Lips, teeth, and tongues explore each other's bodies as we move. My soul's on fire. Not only am I burning from the inside out, I swear, I need him more than my next breath. Through every kiss, every caress, and the words he speaks, I know without a doubt this man loves me, he cherishes me, and above all, his goal in life is to worship me in every way possible.

We fervently crash onto the bed with him above me. His body settles between my legs. As he runs a finger through my dripping-wet sex, I pant, "Please, Finn. I need you fast and hard. We can do slow and sensual later, but I've waited too long to feel you inside me. I don't want to wait another minute."

"Are you sure you're ready for that?" he asks, dipping a finger into my tight channel, then sliding it out and swirling along my slick heat as he travels up and around my clit. I'm so ready for him, I might incinerate on the spot. He's fucking killing me in the best possible way.

"Fuck..." I moan in desperation as he repeats this move, one, two, three more times.

I can't fucking think, let alone form words. "Please, Finn. Let me feel your thick hard cock pounding into me. Stop teasing."

When he pulls back, I plead in desperation, "Where are you going?"

"Condom," he says, reaching for his bedside table. Hearing that foil rip is the sweetest relief I've ever known.

As soon as it's secure, that jerk runs his cock through my folds, then circles my clit, mimicking the way his fingers did before.

I let out a strangled cry, hoping he'll stop teasing and plunge into me so deep, I'll feel him for days.

"You like this, Raven?" he teases in the sexiest tone, as he strokes me once more. "You want my long, thick cock inside this tight, wet pussy?"

Nodding profusely as he pinches my nipple, I manage an "Uh... huh." I claw at his hips, urging him on.

Again, he slips just a little inside me, and I revel at his thickness, only to have him pull out and trace my seam with his cock and circle my clit once more.

"Please, Finnnnnn..." I draw out, needing relief. "Fuck, that feels so good... Please... I need..." I'm not beyond begging. I'm already on the verge of coming, and we've barely even begun. "I need all of you."

Placing his cock at my center, he pushes in once again but only part way.

When he stops, my eyes fly to his.

"You ready for me to love you like you've never been loved before?" He inches in a little further then says, "You ready for me to show you just how much you mean to me?"

His words alone have me teetering on the edge for a release.

I'm so fucking close to the edge of ecstasy, it's taking every-thing in my power not to close my eyes and freefall over the edge. He feels so fucking good.

"I love you, Finn. Please make love to me," I pant, then wrap my legs around his upper thighs, pulling him close. With my fingers digging into his ass, I pull him even closer and beg, "Love me. Fuck me. Make me come the way only you know how. I've never felt this way with anyone, and I've waited way too long to finally admit my feelings for you. I've missed you more than you could possibly know."

"I fuckin' love it when you talk like that, sweetness." Plunging deep, he pistons in and out, taking me higher and higher. Squeezing my legs around his, I hold on for as long as I can before my spine tingles, and my eyes squeeze shut.

The sounds we make are beyond words as I trip over the edge and plummet into a state of euphoria I've only heard of. Wave after wave of pleasure rips through me, and I swear I dislocate from my body and float in the sky above us as he stills and empties himself into me.

The last words I remember before leaving this world are, "You've ruined me for all others."

Chapter 19
Finn

I'm riding the highest of highs as I step onto the stage at the Seaside Music Festival. All is right with the world now that Raven's officially mine. We're only playing a few songs tonight, but we're starting off with the song that won Jax the competition last year. "Just Being Me" is a crowd favorite and has been a popular single. It's also the one that made Sloane fall completely in love with him, so it's special for multiple reasons.

We start the upbeat tune, but this time as I sing harmony, it hits differently. I'm connecting to it like never before. Maybe it's because in all my years, I've never truly been in love. My heart fills with emotion as we sing the last verse, and I realize every single word rings true.

I hope you don't ask how fast did I fall
With you by my side, we can get through it all
You are it for me
I can clearly see
I'm in love with you
Please take a chance on me
By letting me be me.

After the crowd settles, we switch it up to a slow song no one has ever heard. We're testing out "Impossible Fears" and from the looks of it, they're into it as much as "Just Being Me", which makes me perform even better.

It's a song about how we're all our own worse critic. It also focuses on the need for pulling yourself up, making the changes you need, and getting back on track. For a fuller effect, Ryker and I join Jax in harmonizing to the melody. This creates a richer tone and a more hopeful undercurrent to the mood of the song.

As Jax hits the final note, there's a thunderous applause. Ryker walks back to my drum kit, snags a water bottle, and downs it before the next song and yells over the noise of the audience. "Told ya this was the right song. We killed it!"

For our last song, "Dating Season", we switch things up and go back to an upbeat tempo that's sexy and fun as hell to play. I've never specifically told the guys when we were writing, but this song entirely emulates the way I felt when meeting Raven. Our relationship was new, exciting, and ultimately life changing. At least that's how it feels each time I think of her now. The fact she feels the same makes my heart soar even faster than the beats I'm laying down. We all contributed to the lyrics, so I can't take credit for every word on this track, but I most certainly took the lead with the concept.

As we start this song, my eyes drift to Raven, who's standing beside her family left of center stage. I'm not sure who pulled the strings to get them down in front for this performance, but I'm grateful. The moment her eyes meet mine, everyone drifts away, and I'm only singing this song to her.

With my whole heart, I belt out the words,

Our first impression was a joke.
Tried to fool me with your rum and Coke.
But I clearly saw right through you.

Then we danced around the floor
and you got me wanting more.
From your lips to your hips
You've got me thinking I've been missing out.

All my life, I've been fine.
Without ever giving of my heart
It was quick. It was fun.
It never lasted very long.
But just one night with you, has made me see
That I've had it all wrong.

Sweetness, it didn't take much.
But with just one kiss and a hug
I know my dating season is done.
I want you. I want more.
And I've never said this before,
Unless it's you, by my side
my dating season is done.

When the song breaks into my drum solo and a guitar riff, I'm forced to break eye contact with Raven. I truly hope she sees that I'm all in. I know time will only tell if we stay together, but for now, I think we're finally off to a good start.

The moment we finish our song, I can barely hear myself think, let alone hear the directions coming through my ear monitors from backstage; the venue is filled with so much noise. I look to Jax, who motions for me to join him and Ryker at the front of the stage.

When the crowd settles, the emcee joins us and looks to the judges of the competition. "So, what do you think about Jax Cartwright and his new band The Ruby Frax?"

James Collins, the head judge, just chuckles. "They're even

better in person. I've caught a preview of their new single and just loved it. I think these guys are gonna go far! So much has changed in a year, hasn't it, Jax?"

Jax reaches for the mic, then turns to look at Sloane with a wide smile. "It sure has. Most of you may not know this, but just a little over a year ago, I was challenged to get up on this stage in the first place. I'd never performed at a venue of this magnitude, and if Sloane hadn't given me an ultimatum, I probably wouldn't even be here today."

The crowd cheers, so he waits for them to settle.

"I want to thank Smashing Waves Records for putting Sloane in my path. Without her, I wouldn't have entered the competition, let alone win it last year. I also wouldn't have gone on tour and met up with Finn McGowen or Ryker Jones."

The emcee cuts in, "Speaking of Sloane, I heard a little rumor about you two, and I think congratulations are in order."

Jax's smile stretches so wide, his face might split in two. "Thank you. The rumors are absolutely true! Sloane's my wife, and I couldn't be happier."

The emcee looks to me and then asks Jax the next question. "Let's put out another Ruby Frax rumor and clear the air for the entire world to hear. Is it true your wife, Sloane, has a twin sister?"

"Yes. That's also true, *and* she's the one dating this lucky guy, Finn."

Puffing out my chest, I'm sure my grin is wide.

James Collins looks to the crowd and spots the Lancasters. Pointing them out, he says, "I can see how everyone would be confused. Aside from their clothes, they're identical."

Without a thought, I'm reaching for the mic and setting the record straight. "Oh, James, they may be identical but trust me, there are subtle differences. After being on tour with Sloane, she's... well, she's like a sister to me, but Raven... well, she's nothing like a sister. In fact, I've never loved anyone the way I love her. So, trust me... there's a huge difference between them, and I wouldn't want it any other way."

Raven's mouth just hangs open as the audience cheers.

The emcee chuckles. "Well... that's certainly how to dispel any rumors. I know I, for one, can't wait to hear your new single "Impossible Fears". I also hope you release "Dating Season" sooner than later. I felt that song deep in my soul and know others will, too."

Chapter 20
Raven

Now that the weddings and festival are over, the guys have been in the studio almost nonstop. They only have another week or so before their studio time runs out. From my understanding, they're close to finishing the album and have plans to release it in September, which means they'll be touring around the country to promote it.

Things between Finn and I have never been better. We're spending every chance we can together. Our schedules are a bit hectic, but like most busy couples, we're making things work. We've even had countless talks about me joining them on tour.

Unfortunately, I can't afford a trip like that. I'm in need of permanent employment and should stick around so I can make ends meet. For now, I'm grabbing every shift I can, but I wish I could find enough freelance jobs to make it my full-time gig.

As it is, I'm up before dawn, working on graphics every spare chance I can around my shifts at Pop's and spending time with Finn. The tips are great, but I've been burning the candle at both ends, and I'm not sure how much longer I can keep this up.

Now, for instance, I only have an hour until my I'm due at Pop's. I'm working on a freelance design for Smashing Waves Records. They've hired me for a test run at making graphics and logos for their new and existing clients. I've been designing all day, but I still need to put the finishing touches to a logo for Ruby Frax so I can make my deadline. With a few more tweaks, I'll be done then I'll send it off for approval. If this goes well, I might be able to get steady work with them, alleviating my need for a second job.

Just as I hit send, a text chimes on my phone.

> Finn: Hey, sweetness. How's your day?

Before I can respond, a photo of a very sad Finn arrives with another quick text.

> Finn: Any chance I can see you tonight? I miss you.

Grinning at his pathetic expression, I quickly tap out a response.

> Me: Miss you, too. On my way to Pop's. If you're not already sick of their food, you know where to find me.

He's been known to pop in during my shifts. He blames it on hating to cook. By the look in his eye as he watches me work, I'm certain I have everything to do with it. I don't mind. I want to spend as much time with him as possible.

> Finn: You've twisted my arm. Besides, I've got some exciting news to share. See you in a bit.

News? What news? I'm quickly learning his exciting news could be anything from he had a great sandwich today to they just picked up a major venue on the tour. He's used the same phrase for both. I have no idea what his news could be.

Me: You're gonna make me wait? Just tell me already.

Finn: Nope. You'll find out when I get there.

Me: Gah... if you were gonna make me wait, it's just mean teasing me about it.

Finn: That's why you love me. (winky face emoji)

Me: I do love you, but I don't have to like you right now...

Finn: Oh, I'll make it up to you and have you liking me in no time.

Me: Sure sure. (face with raised eyebrow emoji)

Finn: Gotta run. See you soon.

It's rather slow tonight. There's a steady line of customers, but most are regulars coming in for tuna casserole. For most restaurants, it's Taco Tuesday—for us here at Pop's Hops, it's Tuna Tuesday. Jo, the owner, makes a mean tuna casserole, and it's my goal to get the recipe someday.

"Hey, Sweetheart," Tonya says to me as she picks up her next order. "There's a tall and tatted man looking for you."

Tonya knows exactly who Finn is but likes to tease me when she can.

With a little more pep in my step, I pick up the order for my table and grin. "Thanks."

As soon as I deliver my tray of food to customers waiting at an outside table, I scan the restaurant for Finn. He's not outside so I make my way into the bar. Sure enough, he's there sitting in a booth, texting on his phone. He doesn't see me so I take this moment to take him in. He's wearing a dark t-shirt that fits across his shoulders scrumptiously, leaving his ink on full display.

Putting down his phone, he looks around. The moment his eyes meet mine, he's on his feet and closing the distance between us. Wrapping his arms around me, he holds me tight. "I've got the best news, Raven! Do you have a few minutes to talk?"

Looking around the room, I make eye contact with Tonya. "Mind if I take a short break?"

"Go for it. We're slow. I've got your tables and will let you know if things change."

Returning to Finn, I ask, "What's going on?"

Shaking his head, he pulls me down to sit next to him in his booth. "I've been runnin' around like a long-tailed cat in a room full of rockers, waitin' to tell you this."

Okay, his Southern twang is out. Surely, it's big.

"Ruby Frax just got the chance to open for Riser on the first leg of their North American tour. Something happened with their opener, and they canceled at the last minute. I don't know much about the details, but we're in! We're freaking opening for one of the biggest bands in America!"

Practically jumping into his lap, I squeeze him in the tightest of hugs. "I'm so happy for you. This is huge! Wait... what about the tour you've already scheduled?"

"Sloane's working out the details, but it's only twelve shows, so we should be able to do a little of both. It'll be crazy but in the best way possible!"

His energy is infectious. I squeal and hug him once more. "I'm so happy for you guys! As soon as I get off, we're gonna celebrate!"

He quickly tells me how they were all in the studio when

Tara, their record label's manager, came in with the news. He explains in detail how each guy reacted. They were so loud, a sound engineer from the studio next door even came to see what the commotion was about.

When his voice returns to normal speed, I finally interrupt and ask the biggest question on my mind, "So, when does it start?"

Finn's expression goes from eager to morose in an instant. Heavily, he sighs and looks at his hand on the table in front of us. "That's the rub. If we take this gig, we leave in three weeks."

My heart stalls at this news. Three weeks? Holy shit, that's soon.

"Hey," he says, palming my jaw and forcing me to look at him. "I know it's nearly six weeks earlier than planned. But we can't pass up this opportunity."

Shaking, I urge, "No. Of course not. That would be stupid. Of course, you're going on this tour with Riser."

Now it's my turn to stare at my hands in my lap.

"Raven. Look at me." When I finally meet his eyes, they're gentle and full of love. "This is *NOT* me leaving you. This is me doing my job and me coming back."

Then why does it suddenly feel otherwise?

"I know." I sniffle, trying like hell to hold back tears as my biggest fear comes true. This is huge for him. I should be excited. But I'll miss him like crazy.

This is why I shouldn't have fallen for him.

Gah... I need to buck up and not be a doubtful Debby. He's coming back. My focus should be on him, not me.

This is one of the biggest days of his life, and I won't be the one to ruin it.

"You know, Raven," he says, squeezing my hand. "I've asked you to come with me. The offer still stands."

"Would I love to go? Yes! But you and I both know I'm not

making enough freelancing to stop working at Pop's. Living with my sister and Ryan in Nana's house saves me money. I can't just travel the country without having a job that pays well enough to get things I'll eventually need... like insurance and shit like that."

"Raven... what would you exactly be paying for on tour? Correct me if I'm wrong, but where I sleep, you will. Where I eat, you're right there with me. You're legally allowed to be on your dad's insurance for a few more years, so that excuse is invalid, too."

"Finn," I plead. "We've talked about this. I won't be that person who relies on someone else financially. I spent years going to school, and I'm determined to make it on my own."

"I'm not asking you to do otherwise. I'm simply pointing out... I've got food and shelter covered. Your sister doesn't seem to have a problem traveling with Jax. Just think... You won't have to miss either of them."

"Now you're just not playing fair," I grumble. "I literally just graduated mere months ago, I'm not about to shack up with you, so I can have food and shelter... come on, Finn. I love you. But I also need to know I can make it on my own."

Kissing the tip of my nose, he says, "And that's what I love about you."

"Raven!" Tonya hollers and points to a couple just entering.

"And that's my cue to go back to work," I sigh heavily.

As I stand to go, he reaches for my hand. "Promise me this conversation isn't over."

"I promise."

THE NEXT MORNING was hell leaving Finn in bed. After I closed the bar last night, he managed to turn my mood around, and we found the best way to celebrate his touring with Riser in bed until just a few hours ago.

It's later than usual when I trudge into the kitchen for my morning cup of coffee. While I wait for it to brew, I pop onto my laptop to check some emails and get started with some design work I have due later this week. I know I won't have much time with everyone coming over for lunch later to celebrate the guys' tour, so I need to get moving if I want to make progress.

When I open my email, I'm not surprised to see one from Tara at the record label. The subject says *Big News*. Thinking that it's in reference to the upcoming tour, I skip over it and go to the one I've been waiting to hear back from so I can finish this design today. After reading through the specs on what the bridal store needs for the design they've hired me for, I feel confident I can knock out this project in a few hours.

When my coffee's ready, I quickly grab one of the largest mugs in the cupboard and fill it. I need caffeine and lots of it if I'm going to finish this project, spend time with my family, and work later tonight.

So I can stay focused on my project in hand, I quickly click on the email from Tara to make sure she doesn't need anything. The moment I start reading, I nearly spit coffee over my computer.

Hey Raven,
I'll have all the details later, but I want to be the first to congratulate you!
After showing the other execs your recent work for us, they were beyond thrilled with your designs. You capture the essence of our brand, and we'd

like nothing more than for your company to continue working for Smashing Waves Records but on a permanent basis. I'm still waiting for something official from HR but couldn't wait to share this news.

Before you ask, I want to assure you, you'll still be able to work from home and attend to your other clients. However, we may need you to hop into more calls or travel to meet the needs of our bands when needed.

I'll be in touch with you about the specifics once I get a contract for you to look at.

Tara

I have to read through it twice to fully comprehend the message. When it finally sinks in, I jump off my stool with joy. "Holy shit! I did it!"

Sprinting upstairs, I fling open my bedroom door.

Finn is sound asleep, lying on his stomach. His muscular arms wrap around the pillow, and the blankets rest at his hips. He doesn't even move as I bound across the floor.

"Finn... wake up!" I shout, crawling up the bed. Before he can turn over, I'm bear hugging the crap out of him from behind. "You're never gonna believe what happened!"

"You've drank too much coffee, and now you're higher than a kite?" he groggily asks, spinning around to face me.

"I freaking did it! I just landed my dream job! And the best part is, I can work from home... meaning I can work from literally anywhere. If the offer still stands... it means I can go with you!"

Pulling me close, he squeezes the breath out of me. "Where is it?"

"You're never gonna believe it... I'm working for Smashing

Waves Records. I don't know the specifics as HR is sending something over soon. But they said it will be more of an ongoing basis, and I can still have other clients!"

"Ohmigod, Raven! That's incredible." Reaching for my face, he pulls me down and kisses me hard. It's filled with so much energy and love, I lose all track of time.

Eventually, he breaks our kiss to look me in the eye. "For the record, Raven, if I have my way, you'll never have to worry about me leaving you again."

My heart floods with so many emotions, it nearly bursts out of my chest.

"I'm gonna hold you to it, Finn McGowen, because I love you!"

Epilogue
Lizzy

Lizzy

One, two, three—it's all down to me.

As the youngest and only single Lancaster, I'm eager to spend my summer in Seaside, Oregon, with my sisters. It's something I've looked forward to all year, and I'm determined to make every minute count. After all, I've only got one year before I graduate from college and have to adult for real.

However, if I want to graduate debt free, I need to work. I have a lead on the perfect summer job with the nanny agency I've spent the last three summers catering to.

I just have to win over an adorable three-year-old and convince her single dad I'm the right one for the job.

Simple enough, right?

Except when I show up at his door, I'm shocked to find he's the guy I hooked up with a few times last semester.

This cannot be happening.

I need this job. There's too much on the line to walk away. Maybe we can put the past behind us and make some sort of summer arrangement?

THE END

THIS MAY BE the end of Raven and Finn's story in *The Summer Proposal,* but it is not the end of the Lancaster sisters' stories. Find out what happens to Lizzy next in *The Summer Arrangement.*

Now available everywhere: https://books2read.com/The SummerArangement

You can also see how Ryan and Lanie's story began in *The Summer Dare.* It is now available, and you can grab your copy today:https://books2read.com/SummerDare

If you missed Sloane and Jax's story, *The Summer Ultimatum,* you can grab your copy today and start reading: https://books2read.com/SummerUltimatum

But wait... there's more.

Their dad, Mark Lancaster is getting his own story. He's returning to Seaside and you won't want to miss his second chance, neighbors to lovers romance. *The Summer I Found Home* is now available: https://books2read.com/SISFOUND HOME

AUTHOR'S NOTE: If you like reading books set in one world, you'll be happy to find several full-length stories for several of the characters mentioned in *The Summer Proposal* already written and available on my website www.amandashelley.com.

**Ryan is a character included in both *Vince* and *Damien.*

Fair warning—Jules will surely win your heart in these full-length stand-alone stories. **

You can also start reading *Zander,* the book that starts The Perfectly Independent series for **FREE** today: https://geni.us/ASDZANDER

ACKNOWLEDGMENTS

First, I would like to thank you the reader, blogger, and reviewer for taking the time to read this book. There are so many stories to choose from, and I'm humbly honored you've chosen to read mine. I hope you enjoyed Raven and Finn's story. If you want more from the from their word, be sure to check out the Perfectly Independent Series.

I'd love to hear from you and your thoughts about Raven and Finn. You can find me on social media, my reader's group *Amanda's Army of Readers*, or at www.amandashelley.com. If you care to share your thoughts on this book with other book lovers, please consider leaving a review at any of the retail sites or on Goodreads, BingeBooks, and BookBub.

I'd like to thank C.L. Collier for being my partner in crime and making the Summer in Seaside Series come to life. She helped make this random thought I had one day, turn into an amazing multi-author collaboration. With her help, we plan to continue this series for years to come.

I'd also like to thank the authors in this series for taking a chance on us as collaborators and taking this journey with us. I couldn't be prouder of what we accomplished together!

This book wouldn't be what it is without my amazing team. First of all, I'd like to thank Mickel Yantz and Cate Ree, my supportive beta readers. Thank you for always being willing to listen. Thanks also for your willingness to talk as if my characters and their problems are real. I appreciate your suggestions along the way.

Next I'd like to thank Sue Soares at SJS Editorial Services. You are amazing to work with. I appreciate your patience and flexibility. I simply love working with you. My books wouldn't be what they are without you.

To Julie Deaton at Deaton Author Services, thanks for making my book pretty and talking me off a ledge. I appreciate knowing your proofreading is exquisite, and my worries disappear. I know that if I make you feel all the feels, I've met my mark. Your eagle eyes are spectacular, and I don't know what I'd do without you.

To the people who have supported me along the way, I'm humbly grateful to have you in my life. Whether you've read my books, asked me about my progress, listened to me talk about my fictional characters as if they're a part of my family, plotted with me, or been my cheerleader, I appreciate your continued support. Please know it hasn't gone unnoticed.

Last but certainly not least, to my four beautiful girls who have had to wait patiently when I said, "Just one more minute," when I obviously meant a lot more than one. I love that you get that I have deadlines and will sometimes keep me on task with your not-so-subtle reminders that "Mom... you should be working" during my designated times. I appreciate your support more than you'll ever know. Even though you can't read this book—because that might be *weird*—for both of us, I love that you keep asking. I love you all more than words can express. You're the reason I continue to strive and reach for my goals each day.

ABOUT THE AUTHOR

Amanda Shelley writes romantic stories you can escape into. Some are steamy, others are sweet but all have strong characters with a little bit of sass.

When not writing, Amanda enjoys time with her family, playing chauffeur, chef and being an enthusiastic fan for her children. Keeping up with them keeps her alert and grounded in reality. She enjoys long car rides, chai lattes and popping her SUV into four-wheel drive for adventures anywhere.

Amanda loves hearing from readers. Be sure to sign up for her newsletter and follow her on social media. Join her reader's group Amanda's Army of Readers to stay up to date on her latest information.

Readers group:
https://www.facebook.com/groups/AmandasArmyofReaders/
Goodreads:
https://www.goodreads.com/author/show/19713563.Amanda_Shelley
Newsletter:
https://geni.us/AmandaShelleyNL
www.amandashelley.com
Website:
www.amandashelley.com
Facebook:
https://www.facebook.com/authoramandashelley/

Instagram:
https://www.instagram.com/authoramandashelley/
Twitter:
https://twitter.com/AmandShelley
Tik Tok:
https://www.tiktok.com/@authoramandashelley
Amazon:
https://www.amazon.com/author/amandashelley
Book Bub:
https://www.bookbub.com/profile/amanda-shelley

ALSO BY AMANDA SHELLEY

If you enjoyed this book, you will be happy to discover Amanda Shelley primarily writes in one world. For a complete list of the series reading order as well as a chronological time line, please visit:

https://amandashelley.com/reading-order/

The Summer Dare

Leave it to Nana to think of everything.

After a grueling semester, I'm ready for a peaceful summer in Seaside with my sisters.

Imagine my surprise, when I'm woken by the screeching sound of a saw coming through my wall, the first official morning of break.

Not only did I come flying out of bed swinging, but I gave Ryan, the unsuspecting carpenter the surprise of his life, when I came wielding my killer coat hanger and all.

Too bad, I was only in a tank and undies and it wasn't nearly as effective as I'd hoped.

Of course, he insists he's only doing his job.

Since it's Nana's last request to care for us, I can't refuse.

However, I won't let a tall, pesky, sexy as sin, know-it-all get in my way of my summer plans. I pretend I ignore him - that is until my youngest sister pokes her nose in my business and throws down a dare I can't back down from.

Kiss the next single guy who walks up to the bonfire - or explain to my sisters why I get riled up over the contractor.

When Ryan suddenly appears, I know I'm screwed in more ways than one.

Not only will my sisters learn my secret, but from the determined look on Ryan's face, I'm afraid he's eager to reveal it to the world as well.

What have I gotten myself into?

As I walk toward him, one thing is certain - *this summer dare will either make or break me.*

https://geni.us/AmandaShelleyBooks

The Summer Ultimatum

Watching my sister fall in love last summer gave me something I hadn't expected—hope.

It gave me hope that there might be someone out there for me and hope that I might get past my misguided fears and finally let someone in.

With my help, Ryan's planning the most epic proposal. I just have to get the know-it-all musician I work with to fall in line to make it work.

Jax is wicked smart, extremely talented, and sexy as sin. But he can't see the forest for the trees when it comes to his potential. He'd rather keep playing in dive bars along the coast than take a real shot at success.

When the Seaside festival has a music competition, I present Jax with an ultimatum that will either make or break both our careers.

I've laid it all on the line, but can he?

https://geni.us/AmandaShelleyBooks

The Summer Arrangement

One, two, three—it's all down to me.

As the youngest and only single Lancaster, I'm eager to spend my summer in Seaside, Oregon, with my sisters. It's something I've looked forward to all year, and I'm determined to make every minute count. After all, I've only got one year before I graduate from college and have to adult for real.

However, if I want to graduate debt free, I need to work. I have a lead on the perfect summer job with the nanny agency I've spent the last three summers catering to.

I just have to win over an adorable three-year-old and convince her single dad I'm the right one for the job.

Simple enough, right?

Except when I show up at his door, I'm shocked to find he's the guy I hooked up with a few times last semester.

This cannot be happening.

I need this job. There's too much on the line to walk away. Maybe we can put the past behind us and make some sort of summer arrangement?

https://geni.us/AmandaShelleyBooks

The Summer I Found Home

Being a pilot is all I've ever known.

I served my country and I'm damn proud of my career.

But sacrifices were made, especially when it came to family.

I've missed first steps, first days of school, and first dates to name a few.

My kids grew up. They're having families of their own.

Was it worth it?

When an opportunity brings me to Seaside, I jump feet first no questions asked.

It means experiencing all those firsts with my grandkids.

With family as my focus and my guard down, I don't even see Faye coming.

She's a force to be reckoned with and has me holding on for dear life.

I thought our ship had sailed, but now that I'm home for good—I just might get more than one second chance.

arrangement?

https://geni.us/AmandaShelleyBooks

Of all people, why him?

He didn't EVEN bother introducing himself, just assumed I knew him from his fame on the court.

I nearly died on the spot when our professor announced we were permanent lab partners. Between his arrogance and the constant interruption from basketball groupies, there's no way I'll survive this semester.

Sure, he's hotter than anyone I've ever seen in a science lab with his sexy blue eyes, cute dimple, and muscles for days - but I can't afford *his* kind of distractions.

Okay. Deep breath.

I can do this.

After all, it's only one semester.

Just when I think my self-control is in check, he does something to show me that he isn't the egotistical, self-centered jerk I thought he was.

How can his stupid smile suddenly make my mind melt, heart race, and palms sweat?

If I take this chance on Drew, will my perfectly laid out plans disappear?

Vince: Book Two of the Perfectly Independent Series

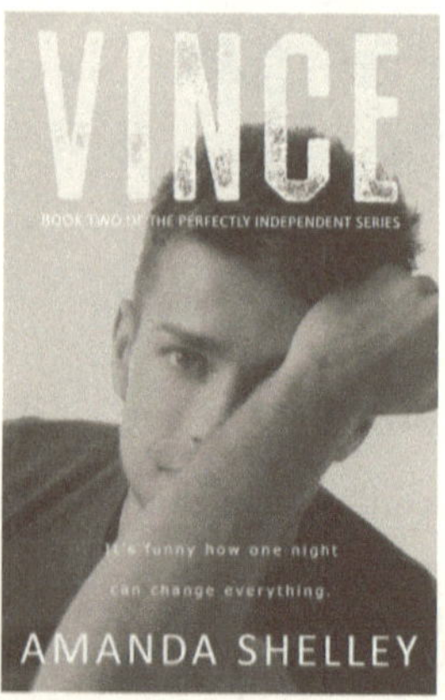

It's funny how one night can change everything.

As a bartender near campus, I'm certain I've heard it all. Rarely a shift passes without some guy taking his best shot, hoping I'll end my self-proclaimed dating diet.

Of course, this is exactly how I meet Vince.

Except, he isn't the one running his mouth.

No, he simply shuts down his idiotic friend, then stops my heart with the simplest of smiles and walks away.

Just when I force myself to forget him, he bumps into me on campus.

Our connection is consuming, and my world is knocked off kilter. It's far beyond physical attraction. He's smart, sexy, and feels like—home?

Wait, that can't be right...

Whatever it is, Vince has me breaking my rules to spend time with him.

My entire life I've prepared for meeting the wrong guys.

Damien: Book Three of the Perfectly Independent Series

Beautiful girls are not hard to find at Columbia River University.

The coeds on campus are great to look at but I was over that scene after graduation three years ago.

These days, outside of being part of the largest civil engineering job on campus, all I'm searching for is a decent meal and some peace and quiet. It's why I'm happy to have found what I consider a hidden gem in the diner I frequent.

All I need to do is finish this job and move on to the next by year's end.

Should be easy enough. Only when Vanessa walks up with a sexy smile and a mouth full of sass, she does more than take my order. She completely takes my breath away.

Next thing I know, I'm here every morning, making every excuse to dine with this intriguing woman. Not only is she smart and sexy, but she's laser focused on reaching the goals she's set for herself.

The more I get to know her, the more I'm convinced she's the one. I just have to find a way to get her to deviate from her perfectly laid plans and take a chance on me.

https://geni.us/AmandaShelleyBooks

Making The Call

Dani

As a bestselling romance author, most assume my life's glamorous, filled with combustible chemistry, and most of all, romance. Ha! I can only wish. With a deadline looming, I've escaped to my family's cabin on Anderson Island to free myself from distractions. My plan's great, until a man, who could pass as a cover model on one of my books, comes to my rescue. Is there chemistry? Sure. Is he everything I'd look for in a guy? Absolutely. But will my career be at risk if I give into my desire?

Luke

For a player, women line up outside the locker room. For coaches, we're lucky to get in the game. As the youngest NFL coach in the league, I live, eat, breathe, and even sleep football. To gear up for this season, I return to my home on Anderson Island for a much-needed break. When Dani literally crashes into my life, my mind's suddenly on the sexy brunette with a sailors mouth, rather than my team's next play. She has me dusting off another playbook entirely, making me wonder, did I make the right call?

https://geni.us/AmandaShelleyBooks

The Boy Upstairs

I ran into Derek while trying to escape the neighbor from hell.

Instantly, we hit it off. Since he's only here for three months and the microbrewery leaves me little time for commitments, it's the perfect setup for a fling.

He's adventurous, challenges me, and he just gets me from the inside out.

With our expiration date quickly approaching, I'm left to wonder...
Will my heart ever be the same without the boy upstairs?

https://geni.us/AmandaShelleyBooks

He Saved My Boy

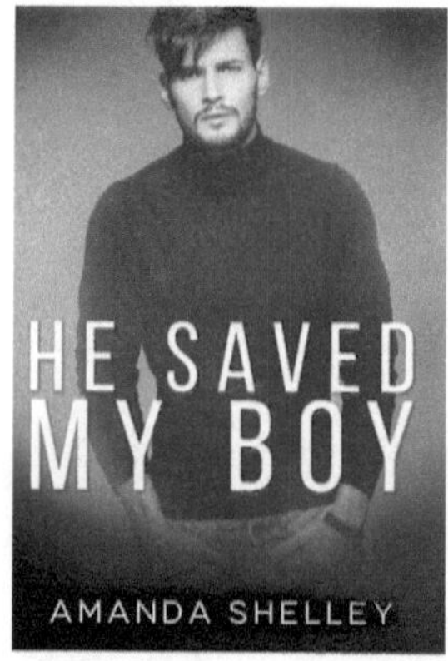

Davis is the first guy to catch my attention since... hell, I don't even know.

Instantly, he makes me think and feel things I've forgotten existed. It has been forever since I put my needs first, so I take the chance and let him light me up from the inside out.

Our night is the kind that will ruin me for all others.

But then I get the dreaded call.

I rush out without a second glance, knowing I'll likely never see him again.

My son will always come first—Always.

Imagine my surprise when Davis walks in, and I find he's the only one who can save my boy.

This cannot be happening—*I guess it's time to pull up my big girl panties and see what happens.*

https://geni.us/AmandaShelleyBooks

The Vegas Pitch

This pitch could make or break my career.

Not only will it set a personal record for the biggest account I've ever landed, but it could set my newfound company three years ahead of schedule for expansion.

Thank god I've got Nate Bellinger on my team.

Even though I had my reservations hiring the sexiest man I've ever laid eyes on – he more than meets my expectations with his hard work and determination. Together, we've formed a solid team and play off each other perfectly.

As we wait for the final verdict, I begrudgingly take Nate up on his offer for a night on the town. After all, this is Vegas and I need to let the chips fall where they may.

Imagine my surprise when I wake up the next morning to find we've not only won the campaign, but I'm apparently married to the man I've only ever let myself fantasize about.

The kicker of it all – he has no intentions of letting me go.

But what will it mean once we leave Vegas?

https://geni.us/AmandaShelleyBooks

Resilience: Book One of Resilience Duet

Resolution: Book Two of Resilience Duet

Samantha never saw Enzo coming.

As the dust settles from her divorce, her life is full. She doesn't have time for distractions. She's too busy running her own company and checking off numerous items from her kids' demanding schedule to have a life of her own.

Then he walks into her kitchen with his breathtaking green eyes and a mischievous grin. He's there to surprise his father - her contractor, but his presence makes everything off kilter.

Enzo's perfectly content with his adventurous life as an elite rescue pilot, until a harmless prank turns on him. Instead of surprising his father, he finds his world thrown off course by the beautiful woman with a sexy smile, wicked sass and the mouthwatering ability to keep him on his toes.

With his limited time on leave, is she worth the risk to his heart?

https://geni.us/AmandaShelleyBooks

Collide: A Sweet Romance

Falling head over heels was the last thing I expected.

Literally.

Coffee is everywhere – and more than my ego is bruised.

When the handsome stranger I plowed into calls me by name, mortification sinks in.

He rushes off to class. I run home to change, hoping to forget the whole incident.

If only I could be so lucky.

I quickly find it's a small world and Gavin Wallace is completely unavoidable. Everywhere I turn he's there. In my classes. Hanging with my friends.

I've got his full attention and I have to admit, I like it a lot more than I should.

https://geni.us/AmandaShelleyBooks

www.ingramcontent.com/pod-product-compliance
Lightning Source LLC
Chambersburg PA
CBHW021715190726
48289CB00008B/2533